KING OF THE RODEO

KING
OF THE RODEO

By

LYNN WESTLAND

WILDSIDE PRESS

First published 1942

TO
My Friend
AXEL LARSEN

CONTENTS

CHAPTER I

TROUBLE HUNTER

" HEADIN' for Camas, stranger? " The oldster reined his horse hospitably alongside where the forks of the trail joined, his faded blue eyes keen and penetrating, a cackle coming from toothless gums. "That's where I'm going myself, though, b'golly, these days it's about livin' up to its name."

"How come, Pop?" The cowboy lounged in the saddle, a big, hand-carved chunk of leather which seemed to fit him from long association, his lean face almost the colour of it from wind and sun. Eyes as deeply blue as Pop's once had been, a well-knit frame which looked to be two or three inches under six feet, a little wisp of white hair among the black, above the right eye. Pop's eyes narrowed.

" Well, yuh know Camas is sheep weed," he explained. " An' it's Death Camas. Way things are shapin', there'll be plenty hell a-poppin' around there 'fore many days have hove themselves down intuh the shadows. That why yuh're ridin' that way, Scotty Stemple?" he added innocently.

Scotty flashed the oldster a closer look, then grinned.

" How come you know me?"

" We-ell, that lock uh hair sort of tipped me off. But I saw yuh ride at Pendleton, a couple years ago. And

I was at Cheyenne three years back, when yuh was what might have been called the big show. Rodeos, they kind of have an attraction."

"That's true enough. But what's going to be so tough about this little affair at Camas?"

"Yuh ever been tuh Camas, Scotty?"

"Never broke trail that way before."

"I thought not. Yuh get around Camas, and yuh kind of get the fever. They've had this rodeo three-four years now. It started out tuh be kind of a little one-day shindig, but first off, the boys from the Curling Quirt and the crew from the Diamond Head kind of tangled. Both of them int'rested in winnin' for their ranches. They're the two big outfits in this section, y'understand."

"Who won?"

Pop cackled, then, producing a gnawed-looking plug of tobacco, he worried off a nubbin with toothless gums and returned it to his pocket with gusto.

"Nobody. That's the funny thing about it. Come quittin' time, both outfits had grabbed off the same number of points. Which didn't satisfy nobody. By the next year they were all set tuh show who was best, and feelin' ran pretty high. Specially after there'd been a shootin' or two."

"Who won?"

"Nobody. With a few others grabbin' off an event here an' there, danged if they didn't tie again. Which left everybody frothin' at the mouth and hot under the collar. The next year the Quirt won, but last year the Diamond evened things by coppin' top honours. So it's still what yuh might call a tie, and this year they're all set for trouble."

" Sounds interesting."

Pop spat.

" That ain't the half of it. This Camas rodeo, this year, is going to be the real thing. No association rules or sissy stuff—not that they have much of it, anyway. Such roundups as Lewiston and Cheyenne and Pendleton are the real thing, but they won't none of them be in quite the class with Camas this year, way it looks. Ordinary, does yuh fork a bronc for the required number of seconds, yuh're assisted in gettin' off gentle and declared a winner. And with other things done, here an' there, tuh see that yuh get out of it with a whole skin. Yuh know how that goes, bein' an oldtimer and a top hand yore own se'f."

" Yeh."

" Well, the preliminary rides here'll be a quarter-minute. But in the finals yuh stick with a cayuse till he throws yuh, or yuh tame him. And believe me, they've got some of the toughest outlaws they could find in the whole West comin' up for them finals. There's Bad Boy, and Sinful Settin', not tuh mention that hoss Wickedness."

" I've heard of Wickedness and Bad Boy, but not this Sinful Setting."

Pop chuckled again.

" Yuh rode Wickedness the required time last year, I recall. But yuh didn't tame him, nor no more did anybody else. This year they say he's a plumb devil, and that he was right peaceful last season compared tuh now. But he's killed a man, and Bad Boy has tried mighty hard to, two-three times. This Sinful Settin', he ain't never been in a rodeo, nor what's more, he's never been topped in his career. But he's killed two men and darn near got a third, all top-hand waddies that's tried tuh ride him. And there's mebby a dozen other cayuses that's right rarin' tuh be in that class.''

'' Sounds interesting.''

'' Interestin' !'' Pop snorted. '' That ain't the half of it. There's the cross-country race as the finals, to three days of hell on hoofs. Real saddle horses, rode fifteen miles, over some of the toughest country that ever laid outdoors. Jumps, and creeks, and walls, old fences— it'll make these old English steeplechases look mild, from what I hear. And with feelin' runnin' high and both the Diamond and the Quirt ready tuh shoot the works, and by shootin' I mean likely just that, 'fore it's finished—oh, I guess it'll be a real nice little rodeo, all right.''

They rode for a few minutes in silence. Off in the distance now could be seen the towering outline of Diamond Head—a massive mountain rising up above the other hills like a giant among pigmies, wooded to near the top, then starkly bare.

'' That's the dividin' line between the Diamond and the Quirt,'' Pop volunteered. '' Each of them owns about half of it. Camas, it's a dozen miles this side. Yuh'll be able to see it soon's we top the next rise.''

Then, as Scotty still made no comment, he ventured another suggestion.

'' Them two outfits 'd pay mighty good wages tuh a top hand like yuh tuh ride in that rodeo. Course, they's a rule that tuh ride for any of 'em yuh've got tuh have worked for 'em for ten days before, at least. And the rodeo starts in two weeks.''

'' Sounds interesting,'' Scotty commented, and yawned. Pop gave up in disgust.

An hour later they jogged into Camas. As a cow

town there was little to distinguish it from many another, save for the rather elaborate rodeo grounds and stands just at the edge of the town. And near the centre of the long main street, two saloons, fronting each other, one with a vivid red front, the other yellow with green trimmings, and both of them unusually big buildings. Pop jerked a thumb.

"The Bucket uh Blood, there, is used by the Quirt and their friends. While the Diamond waddies hang out in the Golden Palace. Makes kind uh poor business for the other places, 'cept when things are stewin' up, as now. Then the average waddie, like me, kind of hangs out in a quieter spot. Where yuh headin' for?"

"Looks like a restaurant there, down the street. Think I'll get a bite."

"Yeh, that there caf-fay, they serve up pretty good grub. Well, I'll be seein' yuh."

Scotty slid on to a stool and ate in silence, apparently unconscious of the glances cast his way by others.

Toothpick in mouth, he sauntered outside again, leaned back against the building to gaze speculatively around. It was still a little early, with the soft, mellow glow of evening just beginning to harmonise the ugliness of man's rather raw handiwork to the cloaked complacency of dusk. Opalescent tints lingered here, with a blaze of crimson seeming to stream from Diamond Head like the fiery breath of a volcano. Despite that seeming illusion, perfect peace held nature in thrall for the moment.

Peace, for nature. And, for the moment, for man as well. Yet all this, Scotty knew, was illusory, a transitory thing of impermanence. Even as he watched, the crimson tints of the sky were fading out to duller, more

prosaic colours; lamps, faintly yellow against the gathering night, were starting to wink on here and there
over Camas, and suddenly an alien note jarred like a
sudden crash of thunder.

Men were whirling, some of them were running, all
started by that noise. Scotty turned slowly, like a man
whom few things still held the power to surprise. He
tossed his toothpick away, stared up the fast-darkening
street.

Viewed so, he was a commanding figure, even though
of slighter build than the average tall man who walked
those streets. His very quietness suggested the poised
alertness of a puma stretched along a limb, and in the
broadness of shoulders, the lithe waist and easy-hang-
ing arms was something again to suggest a puma. He
wore no outward guns—something again a bit unusual
here in Camas. Yet he did not give the impression of
being either unarmed or defenceless.

His Stetson was new, almost flauntingly so, pure
white, scarcely touched by the dust of the day's travel,
set at a rakish angle. The chaps were of white cowhide,
fancy yet decidedly serviceable, and showing signs of
use. A white doeskin leather vest set them off, as did
the silver-mounted spurs below. All a rig to denote the
bronc-topping expert, the rodeo performer. Yet a rig
which belonged not to a man intent on showing off, but
rather to one who, conscious of his position, wanted the
fitting thing both in appearance and service.

Now he turned, walked unhurriedly towards the cause
of the commotion. More than one curious, appraising
glance was cast towards him by the now hurrying
crowds on the street, but he might have been alone for
all the attention he paid to them in turn.

He had been in little doubt from the first moment as to what that crashing noise had been. It had had the sudden impact of a gunshot, yet it was not. It was something much simpler, not so common here in Camas, yet perhaps as deadly. One man had brought a stick down across the head of another, breaking it sharply.

The two had seemed to materialise almost out of nowhere, as though one had been running, the other pursuing. Which, though he had not seen the beginning, Scotty judged now was indeed the case. The younger, seen now as little more than a stripling, had caught up the stick from the street, turned and struck wildly, desperately. And effectively.

The club had flattened the bigger man's hat and, despite the protection afforded by it, had felled him like a clubbed ox. For a moment he had lain prone in the dust. Now, after a moment of sitting up dazedly, he was rising slowly to his feet, eyes fixed on the younger man—rising so slowly as to make the whole thing impressive and ominous.

The crowd had gathered, watching expectantly; no one, at least for the moment, made any move to interfere. The younger hombre had stood his ground, making no effort to run after felling the bigger man. Yet it was plain to Scotty that he was scared, badly scared. He studied him with a closer interest.

He was really only a kid, perhaps seventeen, and slight for his age. He wore no gun, and despite his fright he waited defiantly. The other man outweighed him by at least sixty pounds, and was big, thick-built, beefy, with heavy coarse brown hair hanging over little greenish eyes. And now his face was covered with blood, distorted by a look of ferocity scarcely human. And his big, ham-like paws were reaching out hungrily, even as he stood up.

"That's Tollard—of the Diamond. He'll break the kid in two—and nobody dares to have any truck with him." Scotty, without turning his head, was aware that Pop was beside him again. "The kid's Mart Sullivan, of the Quirt. Too bad for him there ain't any Quirt men in town now. Not many Diamond men, either—but most folks like their health too well tuh mix in with a scrap between them two outfits."

The boy was standing his ground, yet shrinking a little despite himself as Tollard began moving towards him. He cast a quick glance around, saw that the crowd hemmed him in now, past any chance to run even if he had wanted to. Then, moving with deceptive quickness, Tollard grabbed him.

Huge paws closed on the boy's shoulders, fastened with the relentless grip of a steel trap. The boy's face had gone dead white, he sent one glance of agonised appeal towards the onlookers, but he did not cry out. Then Tollard's fingers were moving, like the engulfing, never-loosening jaws of a bulldog, towards his throat.

He had got his grip now. And Scotty saw with incredulity what he intended. Simply to increase that pressure, not merely to shut off the boy's wind but, it appeared, to snap his neck for him. The stark fear in the boy's eyes testified to his knowledge of his peril, yet his own fists were futile things, beating against the ape-like chest in front of him. And still, as though gripped in a trance, no one moved to interfere.

"That will be enough, Tollard. Let go of him!"

Men stared at Scotty. The half-dozen steps which

had carried him forward had been so swift and smooth that he had seemed almost to glide. And though his voice was not raised, there was something about it which seemed almost to crackle in the silence.

Tollard looked up, his eyes showing faint surprise and resentment, but he made no move to obey. The heavy guns which swung in the twin tied-down holsters at his hips had a well-worn look, and Scotty guessed that, either in physical prowess or with hot lead, no one cared to contest with him or risk arousing his wrath, hoping that he would stop short of murdering the boy.

A quick glance into the half-glazed eyes of Sullivan told Scotty that that relentless pressure was far more deadly than it looked to be. There was only one thing to do, and he did it. One swift motion, and he had one of Tollard's guns boring hard into Tollard's stomach.

"Let go of him!" he repeated.

CHAPTER II

DIAMOND MEN

INCREDULITY, anger, blended in Tollard's fishlike eyes, but he obeyed. Sullivan staggered back, his throat showing livid marks, his breath coming in a hoarse wheeze. There was a choked cry, and Scotty had a glimpse of a girl pushing breathlessly through the crowd and up to Sullivan, an arm thrown protectingly about his shoulders. But he had no time then for distracting elements.

The incredulity had faded from Tollard's eyes, leaving a stark rage which was terrible in its intensity. His hands half-moved towards Scotty, hesitated as the gun nudged him more sharply.

"I wouldn't, not if I was you," Scotty warned softly. "You'd have killed him in another minute."

"I'll kill you, you——"

"Easy now," Scotty warned. "There's a lady present. And I'm holdin' the gun."

The warning penetrated to Tollard's rage-fogged brain. He drew back a little, his eyes never leaving Scotty's face.

"Yuh win—this time," he grunted. "Yuh givin' me back my gun?"

"Sure. Why not?" Scotty twirled it once, thrust it back into its holster, while some of the onlookers gasped, noting that he packed no visible weapon himself. For a moment the big man stared at him as though undecided. Then he turned and shouldered roughly through the crowd, which all at once was dissolving as though it had urgent business elsewhere. Scotty was aware that the girl and Sullivan were at his shoulder.

"Mister, I—I can't ever thank yuh——" Sullivan began. "He—he sure aimed tuh kill me——"

The girl had been sweeping Scotty with clear grey eyes which seemed to miss no detail. Deep eyes, set wide apart under softly curling hair, the colour of new-washed gold. Now she spoke.

"We do thank you, Mr. Stemple. I'm Dawn Sullivan and this is my brother, Marty. I do think that Tollard might have killed him—he's killed more than one man, and because everybody is afraid of him, and of the Diamond, he gets away with it.''

There was an underlying tinge of bitterness to her voice, scorn in the glance she sent towards the others now hastily seeking the shelter of nearby buildings, as though caught in some sort of mischief.

"He seemed rougher than was necessary, for a fact,'' Scotty agreed. "Anyway, he's too big to pick on Mart, here, that way. How come he was so wrought up, Mart ? "

"I'd just ridden into town, and was on the back street here,'' Mart Sullivan explained. "There's a big puddle of mud back there, and I didn't see him at all, for he was standin' kind of behind his horse. Then he stepped out, and my horse kicked mud on him. He jerked me out of the saddle before I hardly knew what was going on, but I managed to break loose and run. Then he was after me, and I—well, you saw it, I guess.''

"I saw it," Scotty agreed dryly.

"And you were the only man with nerve enough to go up against him,'' Dawn added a little breathlessly. "But I'm afraid you've made a bad enemy. He's relentless, and he's pretty terrible, besides being a rider for that terrible Diamond Head outfit.'' Her eyes were again appraising him swiftly. "You are Scotty Stemple, aren't you ? "

"Happens I am.''

"Well—if you're going to stick around here any—why not work for the Quirt ? You can go to work now for the Quirt, and that will make you eligible for the rodeo. Which will be right in your line, and pay you good money, too. And with the Quirt behind you,

B

you won't need to worry about those killers on the Diamond."

Scotty was staring back at her, seeing the eagerness in her brother's eyes, and for once he found himself at a loss for words. The dusk was claiming the street, yet still leaving light enough to see at close range. While Scotty hesitated someone approached, boots clattering loud on the board sidewalk, then turned suddenly, a warm hand had caught Scotty's and was gripping it very hard.

"Well, here yuh are, Scotty, yuh old son-of-a-gun! Gosh, but I'm glad tuh see yore homely mug again! Been lookin' for yuh! Yuh're a sight for sore eyes, hang my hide on a barbed wire fence if yuh ain't! When 'd yuh get in?"

"About an hour ago, Fatty." Scotty's grip was as hearty, his own face beaming with pleasure. He and Fatty Brine had ridden more than one range together, and it had been directly due to Fatty's representations that he was here in Camas to-night. For Fatty Brine was a man to ride the mountain with.

Big, bow-legged, shapeless, Fatty looked anything but what he was. Graceful on foot as a duck out of water, he was in his natural element when in the saddle. There was no better cowboy for all-round work to be found in a dozen states, as Scotty well knew.

"The Old Man was tickled a baby-blue pink when he found yuh'd take the job of hoss wrangler on the Diamond," Fatty continued enthusiastically. "And knowin' that yuh'd be here in time tuh ride in the rodeo just plumb made him fit tuh lift himself by his bootstraps—and he's heftier than me, at that. But yuh ridin' for the Diamond, on that Ten-Spot hoss of yore's

—why, them Quirt hombres won't have half as much chance as an icicle in the Old Nick's mouth.''

For a moment, genuinely delighted to see Fatty again, Scotty had given no thought to Dawn Sullivan or her brother. Now he glanced up to see that they had retreated a little way, were eyeing him queerly—glancing from behind with mingled feelings to Fatty with open distaste. Then they had turned and were gone in the gloom.

Fatty stared after them for a moment, glanced back at Scotty.

" That gal been playin' up to yuh, tryin' tuh get yuh to ride for the Quirt ? " he demanded suspiciously.

" Why, yes, she did offer me a job on the Quirt,'' Scotty nodded.

The hostility in Fatty's eyes increased.

" Can yuh beat that ? " he growled. " Course, with yuh famous as yuh are, and that patch uh white hair tuh help identify yuh, everybody's thinkin' rodeo, these days, and they recognised yuh right off. But for plain, unadulterated gall, I think Jeff Odom's got the potato medal comin' tuh him, sendin' a pretty gal around tuh try and grab yuh off for the Quirt ! ''

" She seems like a nice girl,'' Scotty ventured mildly.

Fatty snorted, unimpressed.

" She's a Quirt,'' he growled, as though that was sufficient indictment for anyone. " Kind uh took the wind out of her sails, when she found yuh knew me and was already signed for the Diamond. She won't have no use for yuh now—if that's worryin' yuh any, Scotty.''

" Why should it ? " Scotty asked, but, even as he said it, he knew he couldn't quite mean the words.

Dawn Sullivan—that was a mighty nice name, and it looked to him like it just fitted her. And she hadn't been doing any intriguing for the boss of the Curling Quirt, as Fatty had erroneously supposed.

But for the moment Scotty wasn't anxious to go into details.

He had supposed, when he had received word from Fatty a few weeks before about this job, that it would be just a good job with a chance to do a bit of rodeo riding on the side and, much more important to him, a chance to side Fatty again. But the way things had been happening in the hour since he had arrived in Camas, they seemed to be getting rather complex already.

Fatty was heading for the Golden Palace and, rather absently, Scotty followed him. A hush fell as Fatty pushed open the swinging doors, barging in headlong, with Scotty beside him. Scotty saw why. Tollard was standing by the bar, a dozen others were scattered about the big, rather ornate room.

Tollard turned slowly, his greenish eyes fixing on Scotty with the intentness of a perturbed grizzly's. Unaware that anything was wrong, Fatty was marching straight up to the bar. He clapped Tollard boisterously on the back.

"Here's the hombre I was tellin' yuh about, Tollard," he called out. " My old sidekick, Scotty Stemple. He ain't so big, but neither's a stick of dynamite—but they both pack an awful wallop. And what we won't do tuh them Quirts, with him ridin' the rodeo——"

He stopped, becoming aware for the first time that something wasn't quite right. Tollard's face had gone a little blank.

" Yuh say yuh're Scotty Stemple—ridin' for the Diamond ? " he demanded.

"That's the size of it," Fatty nodded. "And the best rider yuh ever saw fork a cayuse, bar none. Shake hands with each other."

Scotty was waiting, quietly watchful. Tollard stared at him a moment longer, swung back to the bar without a word. Fatty was about to speak but, catching Scotty's eye, desisted. They turned, walked out of the room. Not until they were in the saddle and turning towards the sprawling bulk of Diamond Head, showing vast under the rising moon, did either speak. Then Fatty exploded.

" What the devil is this all about, Scotty ? Yuh hombres met before ? He didn't seem any too well pleased."

"Just before you came he tried to kill Mart Sullivan. I didn't like the idea, so I took his gun and jammed it into his stomach. I guess he wasn't any too pleased, like you say."

Fatty stared, his jaw sagging for a moment. Then he closed it with a snap. The edges of a grin creased his mouth.

" Yuh did that to Tollard, eh ? Only man in this country that'd have the nerve. Well, I ain't worryin' none about that—I never did like him much."

He grinned openly for a moment, then sobered.

" I don't need tuh tell yuh anything, Scotty. I know you. And since yuh're both Diamond men mebby Tollard'll overlook it—public. Sorta looked like he might. But he's like an elephant—he never forgets nor forgives. And aside from yore own self, he's the most all-around dangerous man I ever met up with."

CHAPTER III

RED-HEADED HOMBRE

THE cowboy made no comment. It was a little disconcerting to find that he had had a run-in with a Diamond man, but he knew that under similar circumstances he'd do the same again. After all, he was hired at the Diamond Head as horse wrangler, and the matter of his relations to another member of the crew didn't particularly matter.

The moon had risen by the time they reached the ranch, and Scotty's eyes brightened a little at sight of the group of buildings nestling at the foot of Diamond Head. A sprawling, comfortable log house, a big barn, corrals, bunkhouse and other buildings—nothing unusual there. But the setting, with the bulk of the hill behind, tall cottonwoods at the side and a small creek slipping through the edge of the corrals and on through well-kept grounds by the big house, all added a different, homelike note all too frequently lacking.

Most of the crew had gone to bed. Old Man Carter, Scotty gathered, was a good man to work for, one who inspired the confidence and liking of his men. But he expected hard work and plenty of it in return for good wages and good working conditions. Drones were not tolerated on the Diamond. A man could do the work or he could ride on.

With daylight Scotty had a chance to meet his new comrades. The Diamond Head was a big outfit, its range stretching for mile on mile, its cattle covering the hills. Tollard had returned during the night and, though he had said nothing, nor had Scotty nor Fatty, somehow the news of the new horse wrangler's clash with the big man had become known.

Most of the crew seemed a likeable crowd, accepting Scotty at face value on Fatty's recommendation. His reputation as a rodeo star was well known, and if he could help to win laurels for the Diamond Head, nothing else mattered. Tollard, it was easy to see, was not a general favourite.

Breakfast over, Old Man Carter appeared as Scotty was stepping outside. He was a little man, despite Fatty's characterisation of his carrying weight, and Scotty could see that he carried it by virtue of personality. Not over five feet six in high-heeled boots, with trimmed, greying goatee and moustache and wide-brimmed hat, Scotty placed him as a Kentuckian of the old school. Those shrewd bright eyes, the one long-barrelled gun he carried, told that the boss of the Diamond Head was not a man to trifle with. He would be a fast friend, a relentless enemy.

He held out his hand, appraising Scotty shrewdly, led the way back to the big house, motioning with a jerk of the head for Fatty to follow and, in his office, passed a box of long black cigars. Fatty took one, but Scotty declined.

"A pipe is as far as I go," he explained.

Carter nodded, tossed out a pouch of fine-cut.

"Burley, right from Kaintucky, suh," he explained.

"I know where it was grown, and finer tobacco is not

to be had. What's this I hear about your little—difficulty, with Ike Tollard ? "

"I don't know that you'd call it a difficulty, exactly. He was choking Mart Sullivan, and it looked to me like he intended to crack his neck for him. A big man like him picking on a helpless kid—well, I didn't like the looks of it, and I'm sure you would have felt precisely the same."

"I understand your feelings, suh, and they do you credit. But taking Tollard's gun away from him, to jam into his midriff—" Carter's eyes twinkled through a cloud of smoke. "From his standpoint it wasn't exactly pleasant, I should judge."

Scotty shrugged but made no comment. The Old Man's face sobered.

"Here at the Diamond Head we do not approve of such tactics as Tollard was using," he said. "We are not the gang of ruffians and cut-throats which they try to picture us as being over at the Quirt. Nor have we any desire to emulate them. However "—he cleared his throat and scowled—" this is a delicate situation. The rodeo is less than two weeks away, which presents complications.

"Ordinarily, after such actions as yesterday, I'd give Tollard his walking papers to-day. But if I do—well, he'd just hire out to some other outfit at once, for the chance of riding in the rodeo. And for just one purpose, I'm afraid. To try and get even with you. And you're too valuable a man to risk. If he has no added cause to hate you, I hope he'll be fair, rememberin' you're both Diamond Head men. So, bad as it looks, I'm afraid we'll have to keep him on—till after the rodeo."

"You needn't do it on my account," Scotty protested.

"You're not afraid of him, eh?" Carter's eyes
twinkled again. "I sort of gathered that, suh, from
your course of action yesterday. But I'm thinking of
my own account. We're counting on big things from
you in the rodeo, Scotty. Much hinges on it this year.
Until then, keep yourself fit, get acquainted with the
country, and that's about all you have to do. There'll
be horses to gentle after the rodeo, but I'm not such a
fool as to risk my wrangler on a lot of unregenerate
cayuses till after that's over with."

Outside, Scotty frowned a little.

"What's it all about, Fatty?" he demanded. "This
rodeo seems to be right close to a life and death affair
in this section of the country. Not just a chance to have
some fun, but anything else but."

Fatty's nod was grim.

"When yuh say life and death, Scotty, that's just
puttin' it mild. There's bad blood between the Quirt
and the Diamond, and it's all goin' to centre on the
rodeo—and my guess is that some of it'll be spilled
'fore things are over with. Why, some of the side bets
that are laid on this 'd make a big game of poker look
like a piker's setup."

Scotty shrugged, selected a horse from the string
assigned to him, threw a saddle on it, and rode out to
have a look at the Diamond. His own horse, Ten Spot,
which came just short of being a pinto, was in the barn
enjoying oats to-day and a life of luxury. Not too much
luxury, of course, for Ten Spot mustn't get fat or
overtrained, but Scotty intended to have him in top
shape for that cross-country race which was the big

finale of the rodeo. He knew Ten Spot, and if any other horse won the race, it would be *some* horse, in his private opinion.

It was high noon when, miles from the ranch house, he rounded the corner of a hill and pulled up suddenly, his eyes narrowing. Not fifty feet ahead a couple of horses cropped the grass unconcernedly, reins dragging. Near them were two people who were far from unconcerned.

One of them was Dawn Sullivan, her eyes flashing, face flushed, hair dishevelled. Before her, half laughing, half angry, was a man whose supreme confidence in his control of the situation angered Scotty unreasonably. He was a big man, standing what looked to be an even six feet, smooth shaven, with red hair and a prominent nose but, for all that, handsome as the devil. Now he laughed suddenly and moved as swiftly, his long arms reaching out for Dawn.

Neither of them had seen Scotty. Dawn cried out, was struggling in his arms. And in that moment Scotty's horse had crossed the intervening space, he was out of the saddle and had jerked the man around with a heavy hand.

"Take your paws off her!" he grated.

For a moment the red-haired man stared at him unbelievingly. Then swift fury mounted in his face, like a black cloud rolling over the mountain, and without a word he lunged forward, big fists flailing.

Scotty was suddenly calm and cool again. He didn't understand himself, to lose his temper that way, or to go interfering so suddenly, but it had happened. And if this hombre wanted a licking, he was in just the mood to give it to him.

Sidestepping the first wild rush, he aimed a blow as the other man lunged by, but missed in turn. Then they had closed, neither giving ground, fighting hard, brutally, while the girl stood back a little way and watched with wide eyes.

"So you want trouble, do you?" the redhead ground out, and bit the word off on a short howl of pain as Scotty's fist, catching him on the open mouth, gave Scotty a broken knuckle and caused his opponent to spit blood. "Well, damn you," he panted. "You'll sure get it!"

Scotty said nothing. His own muscles were like whip cords, and he was no stranger to this sort of thing. And while he had discovered in a hurry that this man would be no mean opponent, it had always been his theory that the bigger they came, the harder they fell. All you had to do was outlast them.

A stone turned under his foot, sending him sprawling. He rolled, alert for a kick or a jump, but the other man was waiting for him to get up again, making no effort to take advantage of his bad luck or to fight foul. Scotty's eyes warmed a little. Here was an opponent he could respect, even like, under other conditions.

Dawn cried something which was lost as they came together again. Then, so furious was the fight that again she could do nothing but watch. The battle could not last long at such a pace. Both men were giving and taking a lot of punishment. And this fellow was one tough hombre, Scotty admitted to himself ungrudgingly. He allowed a fist to catch him full in the face, jarring him, but found the opening he wanted, slid his own fist past and to the point of the chin, his whole weight behind it. He saw the big man go down, rocked off his feet, sprawl with a dazed light in his eyes, unable to get up despite his try.

He was game, Scotty admitted. Game all the way through. And in a few minutes, if Scotty stuck around, he would be just bull-headed enough to want to resume, principally because the girl had seen him take that licking. Scotty turned to his horse, swung back into the saddle. He didn't want to have to hit him again. His anger, so hot at the start, had run out, leaving him cold.

If he looked at Dawn again, spoke to her—well, he could easy get all hot again. And she could get along all right now. Likely he'd made enough of a fool of himself for one day. He seemed to be wading into trouble plenty often since coming to the Camas country.

Though he knew that Dawn was still staring at him, wide-eyed and a little expectantly, Scotty rode away without a word. Which was a harder job than the fight had been.

There'd be questions, of course, back at the bunkhouse. With one eye half closed, knuckles broken and other signs of trouble, he could count on Fatty demanding an explanation, if no one else did. Well, all he hoped was that he hadn't tangled with another Diamond man. He had seen most of the crew, but not all of them, so he couldn't be sure even on that count.

Fatty, as he had expected, was as full of curiosity as a hen of cackles, and was not to be denied nor put off.

"Just a little run-in I had with another hombre," Scotty temporised. "And if you think I look bad, you'd ought to see him."

"Yes, I know all that—knowin' you, Scotty." There was a seriousness about Fatty which was alien to his usual easy-going nature. " But danged if I don't begin tuh think I made a mistake gettin' yuh up to this country in the first place. Usual you're plumb peaceful, but here yuh seem tuh be stickin' yore neck out. Give uncle the details, now—all of them."

Scotty sighed.

" I suppose there's no getting around it. You stick to a subject worse than a burr in a horse's tail. It's simple enough. I come unexpected-like on Dawn Sullivan and a man. He was trying to kiss her against her will. I saw red. And so I licked him. That's all there is to it."

" Oh, that's all, is it ? " Scotty was aware that the rest of the crew were suddenly watching him with the same strained attention that Fatty was manifesting. " Yuh couldn't give me any idea of what this here hombre looked like, could yuh ? "

" Well, he doesn't look quite as pretty now as he did before we tangled, I'm afraid. But he still stands about six feet tall, I'd guess, with a big nose and red hair—"

" Red hair ! " It was a wail. " Now yuh have gone and done it," Fatty mourned. " Why, yuh durned fool, do yuh know who yuh gone and tangled with this time, Scotty ? "

" Don't tell me it's the sheriff ? "

" I wish tuh gosh it was. He wouldn't count much. That was Jeff Odom, owner of the Curling Quirt. And if there was unpleasantness between the two outfits before, it's an everlastin' cinch that it'll be war now— and not maybe."

Scotty digested this amid a profound silence. These men were taking it so seriously that he knew that Fatty wasn't joking. The feud was getting worse, and what he had done might well be the match applied to gunpowder. But—well, if they wanted trouble, why not?

"I didn't know about that," he admitted slowly. "But I reckon I'd have acted just the same if I had known. When a man tries to get rough with a girl against her will——"

"Pig's feet," Fatty wailed. "I know what a Galahad sort of a hombre yuh are, Scotty. But this time yuh made a danged bad mistake. Mebby she was actin' up a little—I dunno. Girls and colts have a way of that. But it's an everlastin' cinch that she didn't mean it, and yuh hadn't no cause to go buttin' in. Why, durn it, Scotty, she's engaged tuh be wedded tuh that hombre!"

CHAPTER IV

RED-EYE RESULT

ENGAGED to be wedded! Well, that made it different, all right—a lot different. He'd been a bigger fool than he thought, in a lot of ways.

"Reckon I'd better ride over to the Quirt," he told Fatty quietly a little later. "Mebby I owe him an apology."

Fatty, in process of pulling off a boot, stopped to stare.

"And yuh'd ride over there tuh give him one? Green frogs, Scotty, I don't think I ever will get tuh really know yuh."

He finished removing the boot reminiscently, wiggled a toe reflectively where it played peek-a-boo through his sock and, sighing, reached for another pair.

"Yuh'll more likely find 'im in town this evenin'," he said. "And if yuh insist on ridin', guess I'd better tag along. Yuh kind of need a guardian, way it looks."

"No need for you to mix in this, Fatty."

"Me, I'm in it already. Ain't I the hombre that had the bright idea of bringin' yuh up here in the first place?" Fatty snorted. "If yuh ever see signs of me gettin' another idea, call up the sheriff and have me locked up till it's over with."

Camas was boisterous to-night, and it did not take long to see why, even before they reached the outskirts. The crew of the Quirt were in town.

Fatty reined his horse back into the shadows and looked at his friend.

"Best thing we can do is head back the way we come. It's their turn to howl to-night, but I ain't right partial tuh havin' them do it over my bones. So what do we do?"

"I'll look around a little, to see can I discover Odom. Then I'll join you at the edge of town."

"Like sweet daisies you will!" Fatty dismounted, tied his horse beside Scotty's at a well-chewed hitching rail. "At least I know the way around this town better'n you do."

"If it's a funeral," said Scotty, with a rare grin, "don't blame me. You're hornin' in on your own hook."

Fatty snorted, but disdained a reply. Going as unobtrusively as possible, keeping to the shadows, they looked around, heading gradually towards the Bucket of Blood. The big saloon was humming with activity to-night, and the Quirt seemed to be in a spending mood. Fatty shook his head dolorously.

"I don't like it," he growled. "When they get tuh actin' this way, with the rodeo not so far ahead, it's sure that they're mixin' medicine. All of it bad."

"There's Odom," Scotty said. "Stay here and I'll have a word with him."

Jeff Odom was just coming down the street, alone, walking like a man in deep thought. His face was bruised and discoloured, as was Scotty's, but he seemed to be paying no more attention to it than the horse wrangler had done to his own abrasions. At the moment he was not only alone but in a quiet section of the street. He looked up as Scotty was beside him, his eyes narrowing suddenly. Glancing around, he saw Fatty lurking in the shadows, and jumped to an obvious conclusion—that the Diamond crew, too, had come to town, were looking for more trouble.

Even then he did not run or try to call out. But his eyes were hard as Diamond Head itself.

"I'm giving you just five seconds to get to hell out of here, Stemple," he said quietly. "If you don't, it'll be just too bad."

"Looks like I made a little mistake this morning, Odom," Scotty returned, unmoving. "So I aimed—"

"You made a mistake, all right, but you'll make no more of them with me—neither you nor your scoundrelly crew. And when I say a thing, I mean it. The five seconds are up, and you can take the consequences."

He turned abruptly, stalked off. As he did so, Scotty saw men running out of an alley—several of them, coming for him with a yell. Quirt men. Others were coming down the street, cutting off their retreat.

Fatty was beside him, cool and confident now, his eyes sparkling, as the others were around them. Some-one called out jovially :

" Well, well, if it ain't a couple of them lil' boys from over at the Diamond. Naughty chilluns, to be away from Mama so late at night."

" She'll be worried about 'em, I reckon," another chimed in. " There ought tuh be a curfew, or some-thing."

" Well, since they're here, kind of strayin' around on trouble's range, I guess we better look after 'em, any-way," the first added. " We can't do no less."

" Better be careful," someone hissed from the shadows. " If the Diamond is in town, there's apt tuh be war."

" They ain't in town," was the jovial retort. " Just these two misguided lil' lambs got lost and strayed where they didn't belong. Come on, and we'll take care of yuh."

Fatty looked questioningly at Scotty. The wrangler shrugged. So far these men were in a roughly good-na-tured mood, and determined to have their fun. The best thing to do, since they had walked into this trap, seemed to be to play along. Scotty didn't want to get Fatty into serious trouble if he could avoid it.

With the others crowding all around in a mood so exul-tant as to be chilling, they crossed the street into the Bucket of Blood. A yell went up at sight of them, like the howl of a wolf pack, men came crowding eagerly around. Fatty had an innocent, hurt look on his face now. A look which presaged trouble, as Scotty well knew. But even Fatty and himself couldn't do much against such odds, Scotty realised.

c

" So this is the cowpoke that's come tuh Camas tuh
save the honour of the Diamond, is it ? " someone demanded. " Dearie me, I never thought tuh live tuh see
the day ! "

" What do yuh mean, Tubby, about savin' honour ? "
another demanded. " Yuh can't save what there ain't
any of tuh start with."

" Well, there's sure somethin' tuh that thought, I got
tuh concede. It don't even pack a gun."

" He packs a wallop, though—as yore boss will tes-
tify," Fatty growled.

Scotty was quiet, alert. This was a hostile crowd, and
could turn ugly with little provocation. Odom himself
wasn't there. Nor would he be, of course. He had
warned Scotty to travel, and when he had refused had
washed his hands of him, if the boys wanted to have some
fun—even if it got rough. But the stubborn-headed mule
might have listened to what he had to say.

" Say, mebby these strays are thirsty," someone suggested suddenly. " We can't do less than give 'em a
drink."

Fatty's eyes rolled, but Scotty nudged him in the ribs.
It might be dangerous to drink, but it could be more so to
refuse.

" Beer," said Fatty.

" Beer," Tubby sighed. " Listen tuh him ! My chee-
ild, they don't serve temp'rance drinks on this side of
the street."

Whisky, straight, was set before them. Scotty took
his unemotionally, but he saw the light in Fatty's eyes,
saw his face change almost as soon as it was down. Despite his warning glance, Fatty reached for the bottle.

For liquor was something which Fatty couldn't hold.

He knew his weakness, and he left it alone. But, given a drink, especially of fiery spirits, and his control snapped. In about two minutes Fatty would be in a truculent mood.

It hardly seemed that long. He reached for the bottle a third time, in a sudden watchful silence on the part of the gathered crew of the Quirt. But even his action then took Scotty by surprise. When he was liquored up Fatty was unpredictable.

He turned, surveying them, collectively and in turn, much as though they had been a bunch of polecats which he had unexpectedly stumbled upon.

" Yuh hombres think yuh're damn' smart," he growled. " But I think yuh're a bunch of dirty so-and-so's."

With a sudden swing he flung the bottle, catching Tubby beside the head and dropping him as though hit by a club. Fortunately the flask did not splinter as it struck.

For an instance there was silence. Even Fatty looked a little frightened and half-sobered by what he had done. But that had been enough. From a roughly boisterous mood, the Curling Quirt men were in a frenzy. The insult, coupled with this wanton attack on one of the most good-natured and best-liked of their companions, was more than enough to turn the scales.

Scotty reached for a convenient bungstarter, but even with that he knew that they had no chance. Before he could swing into action they were overwhelmed by sheer weight of numbers. Fatty had tried desperately to go for his gun. But Fatty wasn't fast with a weapon, which to-night was something to be thankful for. His act, however, served only to increase the fury of the Quirt.

Everyone was trying to get at them, to kick or strike. Beaten to his knees, Scotty tried to fight back, saw the bungstarter in the hands of someone else, descending. Then the world—or his head—seemed to explode, the lights go out in a blinding flame which settled to heavy, throbbing blackness. His last conscious thought was that they'd be mighty lucky if they weren't beaten to death or lynched.

Consciousness returned slowly, a hazy, throbbing world materialised around him, which seemed to reel and spin. The infuriated roar of the mob was silenced, a cool breeze blew across his face, something cool and soothing was on his head.

Painfully Scotty opened his eyes, lay for a moment staring. Then he understood, in part. He was outdoors, somewhere. Lying with his head in a lap—Dawn Sullivan's lap, and she was wiping the blood from his face with a wet handkerchief. He heard a little choked cry in her throat as his eyes opened, and he sighed and closed them again. Lips which seemed stiff and puffy formed words.

"For this—it was worth it."

CHAPTER V

BROKEN ROPE

THERE was blood on the moon. Only, as the Old Man said, the sign wasn't right just yet. On the Diamond the next morning he had spoken bluntly and forcefully.

" Them polecats are askin' for trouble, and believe me, they're going to get it—plenty! But like Scotty and Fatty say, this is not the time or place for it, and I want you to keep that in mind—if you want to keep on drawin' money on this payroll! We'll beat them at the rodeo, and once that's done—well, there'll be time then to settle other things. We can't afford to spoil our chances now by startin' things premature."

He was suddenly very precise and deadly.

" We are an honest outfit, gentlemen. We will conduct ourselves as such. A gentleman, suh, is always worth three of any hoodlum."

Scotty and Fatty hadn't been badly hurt, though Scotty had a feeling that that was largely due to Dawn Sullivan. He hadn't got all the details fresh in his mind, but he knew vaguely that Mart Sullivan had come along and seeing what was happening to them and that they were already beaten insensible and in danger of worse, he had intervened, protesting that Scotty had saved him from Tollard.

Certainly, in doing so, the boy had paid his debts. The rather sobered crew of the Quirt had dumped them out on the grass and Mart had returned with his sister, who had taken charge of reviving them. And then, seeing that they were coming around all right, had hastily slipped away in the shadows with Mart before he could thank her.

For two or three days neither cowboy would be a candidate for any beauty prizes, nor did they feel any too good. Fatty was frankly mad about it all, and vowed that when the rodeo was out of the way there was going to be a settlement.

Scotty wasn't so sure. The things which were said

about the Quirt sounded bad, but likely the Quirt was saying just as bad things about the Diamond riders. In fact, that seemed to be the case. Each outfit considered the other as little less than a gang of tough gunnies. And yet it seemed to him that, taken by and large, they were a lot of pretty average to decent waddies riding for both outfits, and proud to be doing it.

There was something here that he didn't quite understand—something considerably more potent behind all this trouble, he had a hunch, than just rivalry between the Quirt and the Diamond. But that wasn't his business. His was to ride.

In pursuance of that idea he brought in half a dozen head of horses, going on three years old, who needed gentling up a bit. The Old Man protested that he'd better leave them alone for a spell. But Scotty retorted shortly that, if he was wrangler here, he'd earn his pay or not take it. And, wise in the ways of men, Carter glanced at his new hand and kept his peace.

He wasn't having any trouble with the new horses, even if they should have been put through a course of training long before. Scotty Stemple had a way with horses, when he could handle them according to his own methods. It was a different cayuse that furnished such excitement as there was.

Sam Purdy, who was the rope artist for the outfit, and a good all-round man, had clamped a saddle on one of his string as usual, swung into the saddle, and found his mount bucking like a fiend without any warning. For ten seconds Purdy stayed in the saddle. Then he hit the ground, hard.

Someone ran out and helped him, dazedly, to his feet. Another of the crew shook his head.

"Ought tuh enter that hammerhead in the rodeo, for a fact. Never can tell when he's going tuh get cantankerous—and when he does, he's as bad a devil as any of them. Never has been really tamed yet."

Scotty was approaching. Now he walked across to the hammerhead, gathered up the reins and was in the saddle himself. Scarcely in it before the cayuse let go again. It seemed true enough that this bronc had never been well tamed, and probably never would be, for the average man.

He was a fiend on four legs, sunfishing, spinning, rearing, trying most of the tricks of an outlaw. But the new horse wrangler was sitting easy in the saddle, one hand waving in the air, with as detached an air as if reclining in a rocking chair. Only when the cayuse tried suddenly to pitch over did he seem to come to life.

Rowelling savagely with his spurs, he jerked hard on one rein, brought the surprised hammerhead up again before he quite understood what had happened. Two minutes later Scotty dismounted from a horse which stood quiet as a kitten.

"He'll be all right for a spell again, Sam," he said quietly, and went back to his own work.

The Diamond crew looked at one another. Of them all Tollard was the only man who had no comment to make.

"Me, I've heard a lot about Scotty Stemple, and how he could ride," Sam Purdy expressed it. "But seein', as they say, is believin'. Seems like he was just a part of the horse—and thinkin' the same thoughts, only a little faster. I'm puttin' my pay check on the Diamond without havin' tuh lose any sleep over it."

Restless as the day wore on, Scotty saddled one of his own string and rode out towards Diamond Head again.

Half-way up the side of the big mountain, his eyes narrowed as he glimpsed a rider hastily dipping into a coulee.

He was a big man, Scotty saw in that brief glimpse, with a square, wooden-like face, and he wasn't one of the Diamond punchers. Moreover, though he had a good look at the horse's right side, there was no Curling Quirt brand on it. So evidently this stranger didn't belong to either outfit. And he appeared mighty anxious not to be seen.

There was something funny there, as though he had been caught snooping where he had no business. He had been coming down the crest of Diamond Head, and there was nothing up that way that was forbidden.

Or was there? Scotty rode higher himself, eyes alert. Now and again he found sign where the other horse had been. But the only thing that struck the eye up this way was the magnificent view spread out below, mile on mile. Arrived at the crest, Scotty stared around in enjoyment.

Somewhere near the top here, though there was no fence, no particular markers, was the boundary line between the Diamond Head and the Curling Quirt. Three miles away, on one side, were the buildings of the Diamond, and nearly an equal distance on the other showed the Quirt. In the farther distance was Camas, like a toy village, and, scattered in between, two or three other ranches could be seen. Creeks, hills, patches of woods, herds of cattle, men on horseback, showing like ants from here, all flattened in the immensity of it all.

For an hour Scotty prospected around, going mostly on foot, climbing among the boulders which studded the crest of Diamond Head, dropping down to the coolness of timber line, where a little spring bubbled out. There was something up here. His hunch had grown to virtual certainty. But so far he couldn't quite be sure.

Still puzzled, irritated because the thing eluded him, he returned to his horse, started down one of the trails through the timber. Where an easy slope showed ahead, the horse broke into a gallop of its own accord.

Sunlight filtered through the trees here, splashing beside the trail, weeds grew occasionally, lifting red berries towards the distant blue of the sky above. The tang of pine was aroma on the air. Then, without warning, his horse was stumbling, sprawling in the trail, the ground was rising up at them.

Action, with Scotty, was instinctive. He kicked his feet free of the stirrups and, hands bunching on the saddle horn, boosted himself sideways. He struck the ground rolling, crushing some tall ferns, sat up and got to his feet again, unhurt.

His horse, snorting, was picking itself up as well, evidently none the worse for the spill. Scotty soothed it a minute, then walked back to the cause of it, his eyes hardening a little.

A rope had been stretched there, taut across the trail, between two trees, and mostly hidden by the undergrowth. Even that part of it which was visible blended so well against the natural background that it was hardly noticeable.

It had been set to strike a horse just below the knees, to cause a spill—as it had done. It had been partly luck, partly Scotty's own quickness of action, which had saved him from being hurt, perhaps badly. A man could easily be caught under a horse in such a situation, crushed, or at least have a broken arm or leg.

He untied the rope, which had evidently been slashed

off a lariat, coiled it and slung it on his own saddle. Although it wasn't likely that the same trick would be tried twice in one day, he rode with eyes alert for the rest of the way, until he was out on the open range again.

Supper over, with the crew gathered in the bunkhouse, he went out, returned and tossed the piece of rope among them.

"Any of you boys know that rope?" he asked.

Sam Purdy had picked it up, as befitted the rope expert of the crew. His eyes narrowed as he studied it.

"I'd say it had been slashed off a Quirt lariat."

Scotty waited while it was passed from hand to hand. The verdict was almost unanimous. Purdy explained.

"Yuh likely noticed this red strand in the rope, Scotty. Not very noticeable, but they're the only outfit I know of uses this particular brand of rope."

"I noticed it," Scotty agreed.

"Where'd yuh get it?" Fatty demanded.

Scotty explained. There was a moment of ominous silence.

"Them slab-sided sons uh sorrer sure don't aim tuh have you ride in the rodeo," Purdy growled. "Seems like there ain't no trick so low they won't resort tuh it, either."

Scotty gathered the length of rope up again. No one ventured to suggest to him that he watch his step.

CHAPTER VI

STEER ON THE MOUNTAIN

WHEN he stopped to figure it up there were a lot of queer things that didn't fit. Such as a man being up on Diamond Head who didn't appear to belong to either ranch which owned the mountain, and his planting a rope to spill Scotty—using a Quirt rope to make it look bad for that outfit while he did it. Was he afraid that Scotty would find out something on Diamond Head— or was he thinking about the rodeo, and placing his bets on the Quirt? Or both? Just where did all this fit in?

Discreet inquiry had revealed to Scotty that there was nothing particularly outstanding or unusual about the mountain, so far as anyone on the Diamond knew about. It was a famous landmark, a nice place to ride now and then, to have a good look-see over the country, and all that.

But when that had been said, it summed it all up. It was just another mountain.

Which, somehow, didn't fit in with his own hunch. Well, there were more days coming—though maybe he was a fool to keep on poking around, sticking his nose in where he plainly wasn't wanted. Which, so far, had never deterred Scotty for a minute.

A good-natured hail announced the arrival of Pop. He was frankly a saddle tramp, doing an occasional day's work here and there, but mostly just riding around the country, covering two or three states in his peregrinations, staying a day or a week at a place and drifting on again before his welcome should be worn thin. Refusing to take a steady job, he was always ready to lend a hand when needed. Annually, at about the time of the rodeo, he arrived at Camas and spent two or three weeks.

"Thought I'd have tuh look in on yuh boys and see how yuh was," he explained. "Back in town they're bemoanin' the fact that yore horses are all spavined, with the springhalt, ringworm and a few other things, and that as riders yuh have tuh use rockin' chairs and sit plumb easy at that. Which struck me as mournful news, and mebby stretchin' the trooth just a mite." He beamed around on them. "Till I saw yuh."

Old Man Carter himself had strolled out to lounge with the group around the bunkhouse. Now he grinned.

"Think we haven't a chance. Is that it, suh?"

"Well, I was going to be right extravagant and bet a couple dollars on yore outfit tuh take the rodeo," Pop explained. "Way it lays, mebby I'll go the whole hog and make it two'n a quarter."

Half an hour later, as though by chance, he contrived to meet Scotty alone at the corner of the barn, and the real purpose of his visit was explained.

"I kind uh took a shine to yore style there in town the other day," he said. "And I've always had a sneakin' sort uh admiration for the Diamond. Why, I onc't worked here seven weeks, which is the longest I ever stuck in one place in my life, tuh say nothin' of workin'. But it sure looks tuh me like the old Diamond's ridin' for a fall."

"How come?"

"Two-three ways. For one, the Quirt's out tuh beat yuh if it can. As to whether they can do it or not I couldn't say, though they've got some good bronc-toppers. But there's a lot uh independents, as yuh might call 'em —though how independent they are 'd be hard tuh guess

—they're gangin' up so that, between them *and* the Quirt, yuh shan't get points enough tuh win the rodeo."

" I'm listenin'."

" And wonderin' why I don't spill this tuh Carter, eh? Well, the Old Man's a danged good cowman, and I like him. But when it comes tuh bein' bull-headed, he can give a jasax pointers, sometimes. Do yuh know what he's gone and done? "

" Haven't heard."

" He's bet five thousand, cash, that the Diamond 'll not only beat the Quirt, but 'll win the rodeo. And there's plenty men 'll commit murder for a lot less money than that."

Scotty whistled. Five thousand was pretty big money, even for the boss of the Diamond. It bespoke the intensity of Carter's feeling in the matter.

" Pop, what do you know about Dawn Sullivan? "

" She's a nice girl," Pop responded promptly. " Been an orphan the last three-four years, tryin' tuh look after her kid brother. Yuh got in strong with him the other days, which sorta means a friend in the other camp, I guess."

" You mean," Scotty forced himself to say it casually, " because she's going to marry Jeff Odom? "

" What yuh done there won't make *him* love yuh any more. But she owns a third interest in the Quirt. Inherited from her dad. That is, she and her brother together do. But since she's of age, and he ain't, she swings the vote right now."

Scotty digested this. It was a new factor, but strangely enough it didn't simplify things, seemed only to complicate them.

Having given his warning, Pop seemed to feel absolved of responsibility and proceeded to sling his blankets in an empty bunk.

There was something funny about this whole situation —mighty funny, and having more back of it, Scotty was convinced, than the winning of a rodeo or the rivalry between two big outfits. So, on Diamond Head again the next day, he conducted a search with methodical thoroughness. If his hunch was right, there was a clue somewhere up here.

It was a big, sprawling bulk of hill to go over, but he was convinced that there was something up here, something which another man had found. That being the case, he had ought to be smart enough to find it himself.

A few very discreet remarks dropped at the breakfast table had convinced him that no one else on the Diamond suspected that the mountain might hold any secrets.

He stopped suddenly, listening. Then, following his ears, he came to a little coulee, slashed in the side of the mountain as by a great knife, brush-grown at top and sides. Down in here, imprisoned on three sides by rocky walls and on the fourth by a couple of poles laid across the opening, was a yearling steer.

Scotty stopped and studied it for a minute. Its lonesome bawl had attracted his attention, coming with a ghostly quality from the depth of the coulee. Its brand showed it to be a Diamond steer and the disordered hair about its neck testified that it had been dragged here at the end of a rope rather than driven.

There was no water available, no bubbling spring in the coulee, but it was plain enough that the steer was not suffering from thirst. After a minute, deliberately, Scotty lowered the bars, watched the steer scamper away down the mountain and plunge out of sight among the timber.

"That's what's called dragging a red herring, only in this case it was a red steer that was dragged up here," he reflected. "Whoever was here yesterday figured I'd be back, and was mighty anxious to make me believe that he was tryin' to steal a few critters—even anxious enough to go to all the trouble of draggin' that poor little dogie clear up here for me to find."

The trick was a bit too obvious, but it was encouraging, in that the other fellow must be anxious to divert his attention from something else up here. And if that was so—well, the other thing shouldn't be so hard to find.

A little more looking around showed him where a horse had come up the trail, and back under a tall avenue of pines, where the ground was soft, the trail was easy to see, with the marks of the calf's hoofs, frequently braced and draggy, to be found as well. The right front shoe on the horse was a little loose, as the trail disclosed.

Scotty's impulse was to whistle, but he checked it, moving slowly, standing for long moments in the shelter of tree or boulder, eyes questing, ears alert, before moving on to some new vantage point. A grouse scuttled through the underbrush, a weasel moved like a shadow. So far he hadn't seen a thing of whatever it was that he sought, but he had the unpleasant feeling that some hidden watcher might be spying on his every move. And if he found something that he wasn't supposed to, there might easily be a bullet whipping out of ambush.

That, however, was a risk he had to take, though he was keeping it minimised as much as possible. He stopped, frowning, staring long and hard at a dark cliff of rock ahead. Following along the side of it for a way, he paused again. Then, very deliberately, he set about pulling aside brush, having all the appearance of a natural pile, yet clearly put there to hide something.

With the brush out of the way a hole was revealed, a yard square, extending back into the hill for some ten feet. All the dirt and rock which had been taken out had been piled on a canvas or something and carried to be dumped in some spot where it would not show.

His eyes gleaming with mounting excitement, Scotty looked around, then crawled back into the hole, examining it carefully, backing out with a small lump of black stuff in his hand. Held to the light, there was no doubt of what it was—coal, and, for that close to the surface, mighty good coal, too.

There were a few traces of it showing on the surface around here, but not much. His own eyes had noticed signs the day before, giving him a hunch. Someone else had seen the sign not so long before, had done this exploratory work, and recently. Someone, plainly, who didn't want the Old Man to know that there was a rich vein of fine coal here on Diamond Head, on Diamond land.

The vein was wide and deep. Scotty was no miner, but it seemed only reasonable to suppose that such a vein as that would extend back a long way, and might be a very rich one. There was one way to find out— maybe. Maybe not, but it would do no harm to try.

He circled, still going slowly, alert to everything which went on, eyes as much on the woods and rocks as on the ground itself. Nearly an hour later, he was well over a mile from there, but perhaps half a mile in a straight line through the hill. Over now on to Quirt land, on the opposite side of Diamond Head.

Here was an entirely different terrain, with no boulders showing, and rank on rank of spruce, instead of gashed coulees and windswept bareness such as marked the crest on the opposite side of the slip. But this time he didn't have to hunt very long. At the foot of a mossy ledge were faint outcroppings of coal again, and presently he found where a hole had been dug on this side and camouflaged again.

This one went in for some twenty feet, but it, too, had struck a vein. The same sort of coal, from the looks, as on the opposite side. Either there was the one vein straight through, or Diamond Head was lousy with black diamonds—unsuspected by nearly everybody up to now.

There was plenty still that he didn't understand, but Scotty knew the wherefore of the steer now. This coal was on both Diamond and Quirt land. There was probably enough on either side to be worth a fortune—under proper conditions.

And the conditions were about right now. Talk had been rife, as he rode towards Camas, of the railroad at last definitely deciding to build through this section of country. It would hit Camas, would probably come right close to the sprawling base of Diamond Head. A railroad that close at hand was, to Scotty's notion, pretty much in the nature of a mixed blessing for a ranch owner. But that was neither here nor there, since it was coming.

There was no other coal, so far as anyone knew, within a long distance of here. The railroad would prove a steady customer for coal such as this, as well as affording means of transportation, so that the mine could be made to pay big money. And while there might be a fortune on both sides of the line, it was natural enough that whoever had discovered this should prefer the whole thing.

D

Scotty didn't know much about mining laws as related to coal, but in this state, he thought, whoever owned the land on top had the mineral rights underneath. So if Jeff Odom had found that there was coal here, he naturally preferred to lie low about it until he could manage to acquire title to all the mountain.

Getting such title wouldn't be easy. To make any sort of an offer to the Old Man would mean an instant arousing of suspicion and an emphatic no. But a man like Odom might have some scheme in mind. . . .

Scotty replaced the screen of brush which blanked away all sight of the hole, and retraced his steps thoughtfully. He hadn't been on the Diamond Head long, but already he had a strong feeling of loyalty for the outfit. He didn't like Tollard, but neither did the Old Man, and Carter, Scotty knew, was keeping him on the payroll till after the rodeo just to try and make things safer for himself.

Which was a white man's way of doing things. Besides, he was drawing Diamond pay, and Fatty, in whose judgment he had a lot of confidence, and who had been here nearly two years, swore by the Diamond.

The thing to do was to tell the Old Man about this and let him decide for himself. What he'd do——

Scotty checked suddenly. Someone else was coming into sight, sauntering up the hill as though out for a little stroll. And to-day her beauty seemed more breathtaking than ever. Scotty cursed himself for a fool. What was Dawn Sullivan doing here? Had she seen what he was about, been watching him all this time? Was she connected with the mystery he had already encountered, here on Diamond Head?

To all of these questions the answer seemed more than

likely to be yes. Moreover, she was a Quirt adherent, she was Jeff Odom's girl. It was easy enough to remind himself of all these things. None of which could quiet the leap of his heart at sight of her, the genuine pleasure which the meeting gave him.

CHAPTER VII

DEATH LOOKS DOWN

IF DAWN knew or guessed anything about the business which had brought him to the mountain she said nothing about it. Her smile was bright and friendly.

"Fancy seeing you up here," she said lightly. "But it is a beautiful place to come, isn't it? Up here you have the feeling that you're on top of the world, and above a lot of its petty troubles. It kind of lifts you out of yourself, I think—a mountain-top experience."

"It does, at that," Scotty agreed. "Reminds me of what a preacher said once. That you could stand on top of some of these high mountains and almost tickle the angels' toes. He said a mouthful, at that."

Dawn selected a spot, sat down and clasped her arms around her knees, gazing rather pensively down towards the vast sweep of country outspread below.

"I've been in the habit of coming up here for years, just for the view," she explained. "I suppose I'm sort of trespassing now, but until lately I've never thought much about what was Diamond land or what belonged to the Quirt. I'm sorry there has to be trouble between the two outfits. It doesn't seem right, somehow."

"You don't consider the Diamond as enemies, then ? "

"After what you did the other day ? " She flashed him a smile. "Maybe some of them are, but not all. It all seems so sort of silly and—and unnecessary."

"Looks that way to me, too," Scotty agreed. "I haven't had a chance to thank you for what you and Mart did the other night. But Fatty and me, we sure appreciated it."

"That was nothing." Dawn looked distressed. "Mart and I haven't forgotten what you did for him, either."

Both were silent for a moment, staring out over the wide sweep of valley and plain below to the far-off Camas and its busy preparations for the rodeo.

"I'm worried about the rodeo," Dawn went on. "All of this bad feeling is apt to come to a head then, and I can't see any way to stop it."

"It's kind of too bad," Scotty conceded. "But the way most everybody seems to feel, looks like it would be hard to do much."

"You're riding in the cross-country, I understand ? "

"I guess I'm sort of expected to."

"Have you been over the course ? "

"Haven't quite got around to it yet."

Dawn sprang up and dusted a few pine needles from her riding breeches.

"Then come on. We'll get our horses and I'll show it to you. If you intend to ride that course you need to be familiar with it. It's an awfully dangerous one."

"That's right kind of you," Scotty agreed. Her horse was not far off, cropping grass in a little sheltered spot, and the shoes, Scotty saw almost mechanically, were all tight. They mounted, started down the big hill and at that moment, from somewhere above them, a rifle cracked spitefully, a bullet droned past, just between them.

Scotty's head jerked instinctively, for the bullet had missed his ear by no more than a couple of inches. On an angle downward, it buzzed viciously by the ear of Dawn's horse at almost as close a range, and a moment later the horse was running wildly down the mountainside, bolting in a frenzy of blind terror.

Somewhere up above was a cold-blooded killer, but for the moment Scotty had no time to think of him or of other possible packages of death wrapped in steel-jacketed bullets. Dawn, as he had guessed before, was a natural horsewoman, almost as much at home in the saddle as he was himself. But the sudden bolt of her cayuse had taken her by surprise, and the hammerhead which she bestrode, swift to take advantage of his opportunity, had grabbed the bit in clamped teeth. Now, with head lowered so that her pulls on the reins were ineffectual, he was running blindly.

So far, in the first hundred yards or so of that mad dash, luck had been with them. More by chance than anything else the cayuse had managed to keep his feet. But to do it for very long, with the route that lay ahead, a steepening, twisting trail, would be close to a miracle. And not far below was a spot where a slip would send horse and rider alike to destruction.

Here the trail curved sharply at a ledge, peppered by a patch of small stones which had been sliding across it for years. The drop of a hundred feet, sheer, to the lifting tops of fir and spruce below, was grim. From above, they had a look of feathery softness, but death lurked below them.

Scotty plunged in his own spurs; his cayuse was running almost as desperately, but under control. For a few jumps there was little to choose between them, then Scotty saw that he was gaining. Even as he gauged the chances, he knew that he could not hope to overtake Dawn in time—not on that trail.

But there was a side trail, which her own plunging cayuse had not bothered with, a cut-off which would save some precious seconds of travel. Running as it did between a line of trees on either side, a steep descent, it was little used. Now it would have to serve.

As he turned his own horse into this lane, Scotty saw something else. Not far down the trail, almost invisible where it had been placed, but catching his eye by chance, was another rope, tied across the trail—and if his horse ran into it here, at this speed, on such a slope, he would be in no better position at the end than Dawn.

There was no time to stop or turn, no chance to swerve to one side or the other and evade it. There was only one possibility, and it was almost a case of the devil or the deep sea. Scotty's fingers on the reins tightened, lifting his plunging horse to a jump. Not understanding, fighting the command, it nonetheless was forced to obey, and the trap was being cleared.

It struck the trail below the rope, running desperately, knowing as well as he did the odds against keeping its feet after such a jump at such a place. Yet somehow, with his steadying hand on the reins, it managed to keep going, straightening out.

They flashed back on the main trail just ahead of Dawn's own terrified cayuse.

The horse wrangler reached out and one hand closed on a bridle rein, close up to the bit. His own cayuse was more than willing to slow at command, but to bring the other terrified horse to a stop was not so easy. Twisting relentlessly, they raced on towards the turn and the round stones which littered the trail. But they were slowing as they struck it, were somehow past, both horses still managing to keep their feet.

A hundred yards farther down the mountain, where a grassy glade was peppered with wild flowers which had bloomed and died six weeks earlier in the valleys below, they came to a stop. Scotty took a swift look at his companion, slipped to the ground and caught her as she swayed in the saddle. For a moment she was limp and yielding in his arms. Then she managed a faint smile, a trace of colour returning to her cheeks, and she took an unsteady step or two.

" I guess—I'm all right now—thanks to you," she said. " Though for a moment I thought——" She shivered at the memory, her cheeks whitened again.

" That's all past now," Scotty said soothingly. " Nothing to worry about."

His own heart was thumping painfully despite his efforts to be casual. Cheating death three times in half as many minutes was coming it a bit strong. He saw with relief that the line of timber above sheltered them completely from view of the hidden marksman up on the rim of Diamond Head.

Dawn stood for a moment. Then she turned and, before he was quite aware of her intention, her lips were pressed to his—soft, sweet, with something to the touch which seemed to set his whole being vibrating. Then, laughing a little, a fresh spot of colour in her cheeks, she had withdrawn.

" I wonder who fired that shot," she said.

"I'd sort of like to know that myself," Scotty agreed, his own tone again as matter-of-fact as hers.

Both of them knew that the chances for finding out were not at all good. To try and go up there again now and find the ambush artist would only be inviting another bullet. And whoever was up there could find plenty of chances to get down off the mountain without being seen.

As they were climbing into their saddles again a fugitive beam of light seemed to strike Scotty in the eyes. It was just a moment, and gone again almost as quickly as it had come, but his own eyes narrowed, sweeping around. Then he saw, across and over a mile away, another momentary flash of light.

Over there, mostly out of sight from here, was a man with a pair of field glasses, and it was plain enough that he had been watching them, at least for the last few minutes. Now he was disappearing behind a rise of ground as they rode on.

Farther down the hill, looking off, Scotty saw a rider appear, heading towards the Quirt. It was a long way, but he recognised the man, more by his carriage and the way he rode than anything else. Jeff Odom, boss of the Quirt.

Odom hadn't been on the hill, so he hadn't been the man to take that shot at them. But what was he watching the Diamond Head for now? Did he know something about it all, or was it just a coincidence? There were rather too many of the latter to be convincing, lately.

And how long had he been watching them? Undoubtedly he had seen that kiss which Dawn had given Scotty. Had he seen the cause of it? Or would he figure that it meant something entirely different from what it had been intended for? A gesture of thanks, an emotional reac-

tion after the great stress which Dawn had just been
through.

That, of course, was all it was—for Dawn was Jeff
Odom's girl. Scotty's clenched hands were sweating. Life
had seemed simple enough a few days ago, when he had
gotten that letter from Fatty Brine, telling him to come
along and take a job with the Diamond Head, and men-
tioning the opportunities offered at the rodeo. It had
all seemed a good proposition—then. If he had known
how things were going to develop——

Scotty stole a glance at Dawn, riding beside him, her
cheeks still a little flushed from excitement, or something else. And he knew in his heart that, even if he had
known, he'd have come just the same.

CHAPTER VIII

SIDE BET

BACK at the bunkhouse Scotty had said nothing about
what had transpired on Diamond Head, not even to
Fatty.

The whole thing had too many angles which he didn't
understand yet. Until the rodeo was over the less said
about things the better.

Not that he didn't trust Fatty. Only the roly-poly
cowboy might not prove a perfect repository for confidences just now. Despite himself, and the best of intentions, Fatty was apt to let confidences slip in conversation

with someone else, especially if that other had a bland and easy way of asking questions, and never suspect that he'd told a thing he wasn't supposed to. Fatty couldn't help his shortcomings.

It might be that nobody would try to get anything out of Fatty but, knowing him to be Scotty's best friend and the man who had got the rodeo star to come here, there was always that chance. And Fatty had a lot of good friends among the Diamond crew. Men he trusted implicitly.

Scotty hadn't quite made up his mind about some of them yet. All of them, with the single exception of Tollard, were friendly, easy to work with and get along with. Tollard nodded without emotion of any sort when it was necessary, but he had become a silent enigma, apparently accepting the situation, at least for the time being. What might happen later was another matter.

The next day, following Dawn's suggestion, Scotty took time off to ride the route marked for the cross-country ride, and he shook his head at the conclusion. None of the reports had over-stressed it. It was a long course, and a bad one. Horse-killing, man-killing. It would take over two hours to run it, and only an exceptional horse could stand up under the strain of such a contest.

Beginning at the rodeo grounds, a big circle was completed, out into the hill country and back. There were several jumps—one across an old stone wall which had been built by a sheep herder long years before, intending to make a stone corral for his sheep.

Herder and sheep had long since passed from the picture, part of the never-finished corral had fallen, but at one spot, where a narrowing trail converged on the wall, it was still a high jump and with a poor take-off, especially for more than one horse at a time.

There were creeks in the ways of the runners, and plenty of other obstacles. Not only must a horse be more than an average cow pony, trained in jumping and with a fighting heart, but a rider, to have any hope of winning here, must know his job. It would be a thrilling ride, a grand climax to the rest of the rodeo, counting heavily in points. And with a cash prize of five hundred dollars to the winner.

"Which is plenty tuh buy a new cayuse with, if yuh kill the one yuh're ridin', on such a course," Fatty declared in grim comment. "That is, most cayuses."

"That route, under a stock saddle, would kill an ordinary cayuse or break its wind," Scotty said laconically. "I figure Ten Spot can do it—but if it killed a horse like him, the prize wouldn't pay for him. And dead horses don't win prizes."

"Yeh, that's true, with a hawss like Ten Spot," Fatty agreed. "Yuh got a big advantage most of the others ain't, though. Yuh outweigh a lot of them the right way by thirty-five pounds, and that helps a hawss a lot in a race like that. And yuh can ride."

"Speakin' of ridin', let's amble in to Camas and see how things are going."

"Suits me," Fatty agreed. "Only I'm going tuh tip off the rest of the boys tuh come along. Just in case."

Remembering their last experience, Scotty offered no objections. In town, however, though there was a considerable sprinkling of Curling Quirt men, there was no sign of open hostilities. A spirit of truce seemed tentatively to be agreed upon, unspoken but binding. The rodeo itself would be the time for settlement. Whichever side lost out there might be out for revenge of another sort once it was finished, but now they would wait and humble the other outfit in public.

Already Camas was beginning to take on a new appearance. Decorated in gala attire with flags and bunting on the streets and in every business building, its thoroughfares were busy with the vanguard of the crowd which would arrive within another day or so. The dance halls were full already, the honkytonks blaring and running full time. Gamblers had come like carrion birds to where a kill was expected. And a few riders, men who, like Scotty, had been able to make a showing at other rodeos, were coming in, attracted by the prizes offered and the reputation which the Camas rodeo was already acquiring.

Although a rider must be a bona fide employee of some ranch for at least ten days to represent that ranch, there was no such ban on individuals riding quite independently.

Along with these men were others who were purely visitors, coming for the thrill which they hoped to enjoy. Scotty saw one of them, obviously a tenderfoot, engaged in conversation with old Pop. The range tramp was getting a few drinks at the bar and dispensing information in exchange.

" Ridin', stranger ? " he asked. " Why, by the blooeyed daisies, what yuh'll see at this rodeo can't be matched nowhere else ; no, sir. It's a rodeo as is a rodeo. I remember——"

" Did you call it rodeo ? I had always heard the word as ro-day-o, with the accent——"

" Yeh." Pop signalled the bartender again and sighed. " Reckon likely yuh have, mister. Folks that don't know,

they call it ro-day-o. But yuh take the oldtimers, folks
around here that rides in the danged things, and it's
ro-de-o. Reckon it's all in the way yuh're brung up—
some ignorant folks, from Boston and such like places
back East, they're just raised that way and can't
help it."

With Fatty accompanying him, Scotty strolled over to
the headquarters of the rodeo association. The big room
was half full of men, mostly cattlemen and cowboys,
gathered in little knots. Scotty looked them over. The
Old Man was in one corner, waving his arms and vowing
passionately that the Diamond Head was going to win
the rodeo, and whipping out a big red pocket-book in
proof that he meant it.

Blayley, of the Lazy A-Z, was there, a tall, rather thin
man, boisterously good-natured, declaring that when the
bets were counted the Lazy Azey would be declared the
winner; which was greeted with laughter, for his little
outfit couldn't even enter men in half the events, and
Blayley himself wouldn't even think of riding.

Heads lifted a little, the hum of conversation slowed
and men stared as Scotty walked up to the desk.
Medwick, the general chairman, who was president of the
bank and owner of one of the larger ranches, where he
spent most of his time, looked up appraisingly. Medwick
was a big man, solidly built, with greying hair and the
tanned, weather-wrinkled eyes of a man who has spent
much time in the saddle.

" So you're Scotty Stemple," he said, and arose, holding out his hand. " Carter said you'd be in to register.
We're glad to have you with us, Scotty."

" I'm sort of glad to be here," Scotty agreed. " It
sounds like a good show."

"I'm thinking it will be—a damned good one," Medwick said under his breath. "You're going in for general events?"

"Everything important, I figure on having a try at." Medwick looked up quickly.

"You mean the cross-country, too?"

"I wouldn't figure on missing the main event."

"That requires special registration, with your horse entered as well. We'll be glad to have you in it, of course. Only—well, I'll be frank with you, Scotty, since you're new to this rodeo. Most of the men who go in for the bucking contests stay out of the cross-country. Those others are man-killing enough themselves, and with the cross-country following right on the heels——" He shrugged.

"No rule against it, is there?"

"None in the world, if you want to try it. Though, as for my own opinion, I'd consider any man a damned fool —and I'm not speaking personally—who rides those broncs and then tries to top off with the cross-country, either for the money or the glory."

"Reckon I'll sign up for it anyway. If I'm too bad used up when it comes I don't have to ride, of course."

"Naturally not. I——"

Medwick paused. Other heads were turning as well. Jeff Odom had come into the room, heading straight for the desk. His red hair glinted, his big nose seemed to be leading the way, and his self-assurance was as unbounded as it had been on the occasion of their first meeting. With only a sidewise glance at Scotty, he leaned both fists on the desk.

"I suppose you'll be thinking I'm a fool, too, Dave," he said. "But there'd ought to be room for one more.

You can enter me the same—includin' the cross-country."

"The more the merrier, Jeff," Medwick said imperturbably.

Odom nodded and swung around to face Scotty. If he had wanted to get attention, he had it. Everyone in the room was watching them now, wondering what was going to happen.

"I figure you aim to ride that race, Stemple, or you wouldn't sign for it," the boss of the Quirt said bluntly. "That's the way with me, too—but just to make sure, I'm layin' you a little side bet on that race itself. That I'll beat you in the cross-country. You can name the figure."

Scotty had to admire the nerve of the man. Jeff Odom hated him, and this was his way of expressing contempt, of getting revenge. That last was an open slur—intimating that a mere horse wrangler couldn't afford to risk much money, compared to a cattleman—that he probably didn't have it to start with, even.

"I'll be glad to take your bet, Odom," Scotty replied evenly. "But name your own figure."

"Sure, if you say so." Odom's eyes glittered. "Five hundred dollars?" he said questioningly.

Scotty shrugged.

"Chicken feed. Why not make it a thousand, so the race'll be worth while?"

Odom's eyes showed his surprise, but his face did not change.

"Fine. Dave, here, will hold the stakes. And there's one condition. "Non-starters to forfeit the bet."

Blayley had lounged forward. He studied both of them with twinkling eyes.

" And the hoss that's registered has tuh do the runnin'.
Ain't that it, Dave ? "

" Those are the rules," Medwick agreed.

Blayley grinned and turned away.

" Sounds like an interestin' race," he said.

CHAPTER IX

DAMN' FOOL EXPERT

ON THE afternoon preceding the rodeo the Diamond
Head, to all practical intents and purposes, moved
in to take up headquarters in Camas. A few men who
could not be spared remained behind to look after things
on the ranch, and these would be relieved, at the end of
the first day, by others, who in turn would trade with a
third set for the third and final day. These same general
preparations were going on at all the ranches over the
surrounding country. To all general appearance work,
aside from the rodeo, was suspended for the duration
thereof.

This afternoon Camas swarmed and hummed with life.
Its hotels were crowded despite the fact that most of the
visiting ranchmen had brought along their own outfits,
such as were used on circle, and made their own camps.
From a drowsy little cow town Camas, for a few days,
was a city, rather conscious of its own importance and
a little bewildered by it at the same time.

There were some excellent contenders for honours among the independent riders who had drifted into town purely as such, from other rodeos, and some real talent among the smaller ranchers. But it was freely admitted that the big drawing card, the chief contest, was between the Diamond Head and the Curling Quirt. Because of other competition neither outfit might get a majority of the points in competition, but one was sure to be the final winner.

Excitement was running high over Scotty Stemple and Jeff Odom. The bad blood between the two men, as well as between their outfits, lent edge to the feud. And whereas the Diamond pinned its hopes frankly on Scotty, the boss of the Quirt was easily top hand in his own outfit.

That much was on the surface. Below it there was a lot that Scotty couldn't figure. To stroll around town, keeping unobtrusive and using your ears, it was possible to hear a lot, and the sum total of it was still more confusing.

He knew the reaction of his own companions on the Diamond towards the Quirt. They accused the Quirt of almost every sort of crime in the calendar, from placing that rope in the trail to trip his horse—none of them knew of that second rope—to attempted murder, though none of them knew of that shot which had been taken at him, either.

And on the other side, the Quirt figured his own outfit to be just as bad. How much justification for this attitude there might be he hadn't been quite able to decide. There was Tollard, of course, and his attack on Mart Sullivan. That was about as bad as anything that he had heard whispered.

Mart was in town now along with his sister, and he ex-

E

tended a frank hand in greeting when he encountered Scotty in the street.

" As a Quirt puncher, I'm going tuh have a hard time knowin' which side to feel sorry for," he confessed. " One thing, Scotty, I'll be pullin' for you when you're in there."

And that, Scotty knew, was genuine. Torn between loyalties as he might be, the kid was unwavering when it came to that point. It was nice to know of a few things that could be taken at face value.

In the crowd Scotty, as usual, was alone. He had left Fatty busy with some work that had to be done, had changed to old chaps and shirt which were highly unobtrusive, then started on a private tour of his own. Wandering through the rodeo grounds, he studied things with a critical eye.

A big, high log fence or corral enclosed the main ground on three sides, where the majority of the events would be run off. On the fourth side was a steel enclosure in front of the big stand and bleachers, to protect the spectators from any unruly horse or steer getting in to add to their excitement.

On one end were the chutes, and behind them several pens for horses and steers, with half a dozen rooms for saddles, bridles and other equipment. All in all, it was a big place, pretty well arranged, but offering plenty of opportunity for anyone who really wanted to, to get around and into things where they might have no good business to be. Behind these were a couple of big barns where more stock and equipment would be conveniently at hand.

From there Scotty moved to the livery stable where he was keeping Ten Spot. The pinto whinnied and cocked his ears forward as Scotty came up, questing for a lump of sugar. One of the attendants came past.

" That's a real hoss yuh've got there, Stemple. And he seems to be feelin' right in trim."

" He is," Scotty agreed. " Keep a sharp eye on him to see that he stays so."

" I'll sure do that. I've got a week's wages on yuh to win that race. A lot of folks favour Jeff Odom and his Midnight hoss, but after all I've heard about yuh, Stemple, I figger I'd be plumb crazy to waste money anywhere else."

That, at least, was encouraging. There was one backer who was interested in seeing that Scotty and Ten Spot were in shape for the start. That clause which Jeff Odom had so casually inserted, " non-starters to forfeit the bet," had given him a lot of sober thought.

On the morrow Fatty Brine would be entering most of the events along with him. There was a two-fold purpose in that. Fatty, despite his heft and his uncouth appearance, was a mighty good all-round man, and might carry off some points for the Diamond. That, however, was secondary with him.

" Yuh're a marked man in this here contest, Scotty," he had explained seriously. " And there'll be plenty of deviltry, if the signs mean anything—there's sure blood on the moon. And it won't do a danged bit uh hurt tuh be where I can kind uh side yuh and keep an eye open."

Scotty left the half-dusk of the livery stable, leaving by a rear door, and blinked for a moment in the bright sun. Then he turned at a voice. Jeff Odom stood there, and some of the jauntiness seemed to have fallen from him. His face was grim-set and cold.

" Reckon we're alone, Stemple," he said. " Which

is what I've been wantin'. A chance for a word with yuh."

" Go right ahead," Scotty nodded.

" We don't like each other," Odom pursued. " Which is neither here nor there. I aim to beat you in the rodeo, and after that—well, there's some things that'll require a settlement, and we'll have it. What I wanted to say, though, was this : the Quirt fights hard, but it fights fair. And we'll know how to deal with anybody that tries any more dirty tricks."

He turned and strode away. Scotty watched him thoughtfully. Jeff Odom hated him, principally, Scotty judged, on account of Dawn Sullivan and what he suspected or imagined might be between them. Yet Scotty found himself beginning to respect, almost to like, the boss of the Quirt.

Camas was roaring to-night, and probably would keep it up till long past midnight. Which was all right for those who liked that sort of thing. For his own part, as a veteran campaigner, Scotty intended to roll into his blankets early, and most of the Diamond, on direct orders from the Old Man, were doing the same. Here, a little way beyond the edge of town, the noise came like the distant beat of surf on a rocky shore, subdued but steady.

Scotty was just sinking to sleep when the even cadence of sound was disturbed by something sharper—several gunshots. Others were rousing up to listen, but after a moment it ceased, and presently he heard snores around him. He lay staring thoughtfully up at the dim, star-sprinkled sky above, was becoming drowsy again when there was a faint commotion, and Fatty came up, trying to crawl under the blankets with him in silence. For so

unwieldy a man Fatty could move like a cat, but to-night
Scotty knew the signs. Fatty was labouring under some
tense excitement.

"What's the trouble, Fat?" he whispered.

Fatty turned and, as the light shone on his face, Scotty
was startled. There was trouble looking out of Fatty's
eyes, and it took a lot to disturb this placid cowpuncher.

"What was that row in town? You in on it?"

Fatty nodded.

"Yeh. Kind of a brush between some of our two pet
outfits. Nobody hurt—much. I don't think either side
started it, but they both thought the other did. Tollard
winged one of their men, so's he won't be able to ride
to-morrow."

Scotty's jaw set a little in the darkness. Tollard would
have to do that. And if feeling had been bad before, it
certainly would be ten times as bad by the opening hour
of the rodeo.

"That'll be bad."

Fatty grunted.

"It's bad enough. But it ain't a patchin' tuh what
I found out. The gol-durned old fool!"

"What are you talking about?"

"I'm talking about the Old Man. I knew he was all
het up about this here affair, but I didn't think he'd quite
taken leave uh his senses—allers supposin' he had same
tuh start with."

"What's he done now?"

"Plenty. He's bet the outfit—the whole Diamond
Head, mind you—on the outcome!"

"What?" For once Scotty was shocked out of his
habitual calm. He sat up in bed. "Everything?"

"Lock, stock and barrel. And if they'd kicked up a

rumpus before, there's plenty 'd murder every man uh us for plenty less than that.''

" He's bet on the Diamond winning the rodeo ? "

Fatty groaned.

" Naw. That 'd have been bad enough, gosh knows. But he's bet it that we'll beat the Quirt—not only on final points, but on the bucking and the cross-country. And, meanin' no disrespect tuh yuh, Scotty, but that's about as big a damfool bet as ever I heard tell of—and I speak as an expert who's made plenty on his own account ! "

CHAPTER X

BULLDOGGER'S BLOOD

THAT was bad. And the fact that Jeff Odom had also bet the Quirt, as it developed, on the proposition that it could beat the Diamond, didn't make it any better. Both cattlemen had virtually stood to win big and the other to lose, but as applied to the whole situation, it made a nice kettle of devil's brew.

Scotty considered the situation for full five minutes. Then he turned over and went to sleep. Worrying wouldn't help the matter. There was riding to do in the next three days.

Camas might not have a better mousetrap, but news of their rodeo had spread widely enough that all the world which they could accommodate was beating a path to their door. Scotty wasn't interested in the crowd. He had seen plenty of them before. But the horses which were paraded out in the open for everyone to look at were something else again.

In addition to Bad Boy, Sinful Setting and Wickedness, fully a score of other outlaws had been brought in which gave promise of living up to the name. And there were plenty of unbroken cayuses which could and would give average riders plenty of trouble during the preliminaries.

The pageantry of opening out of the way, the rodeo settled down to serious business in an artistic way. Sam Purdy showed his stuff with a rope, and to his bewildered surprise was awarded second place. The Quirt had imported a new man several weeks before, ostensibly as a plain cow waddy, and had kept the secret well. But when the plain and fancy roping was over, he was hailed as the new champion. Which, beating Sam Purdy, meant plenty.

The Old Man, a big cigar clenched between his teeth, the end frazzled and long since gone out, sat in the stands and watched this exhibition tensely. The Diamond had figured the roping as belonging to them.

" That calf got away," he said to Scotty. " Go in and put our brand on the next one."

The next one was calf tying. Scotty left the stand, moved around to one side of the corral fence, and perched there, watching imperturbably. There were a lot of contestants here, and as it happened, he had drawn last place. Which was all right with him.

Fatty was among the first starters. Usually he was also among the first finishers, but this time he got off to a bad start. With a rope already looped and half twisted in place, a sudden lunge on the part of the calf, a kick, and the rope was in a snarl. Those things didn't happen often, not to an expert, but occasionally they could happen to anyone. Five minutes later, panting a little, Fatty came and climbed up beside Scotty.

"I sure muffed that one," he growled. "Hah, there goes Tollard now. Let's see how he does."

Tollard was doing good work. Strong as a horse, quick and fast. it looked like child's play for him to handle a calf. A little murmur went up as he straightened.

"Mighty close tuh the record," Fatty murmured. "He's way ahead uh those other bozos."

By the time it came Scotty's turn, one thing was apparent. The Diamond already had the calf tying, with Tollard's exhibition.

"And if yuh beat him, he won't take kindly tuh it," Fatty sighed. "Go in there and show him up, Scotty. I'll sort uh watch that this fence don't fall down while yuh do it."

Scotty did it. Did it with a seeming ease and expertness which drew a round of applause from the audience. He caught a glimpse of Dawn, saw her wave to him, felt a sudden pleasurable thrill in the whole thing. Fatty looked at him with new respect as he climbed back on the fence.

"Doggone, Scotty, I've heard a lot about what a fencebuster yuh was at these rodeos the last couple years, but I've always been too busy to pay very much attention tuh such things. But you sure showed yore class that time."

A halt was called for dinner. The sun was high overhead, hot and pitiless, with scarcely a breath of air stirring. The afternoon would be a scorcher unless a shower blew up. The air was already humid, with buzzing, sticky flies making the horses and cattle doubly irritated, chafing at the edges of men's tempers.

Back at the grounds, the routine went on. Late in the afternoon, the preliminaries in the bucking contest would be held, with more to come the next day, and the finals on the forenoon of the third day. The cross-country race, the third afternoon, would be the wind-up.

Much water would flow under the bridge in the meantime. Water! Scotty looked towards the distant coolness of old Diamond Head and mopped his face. The bulldogging was about to start; the first steer was coming out of the chute now, bawling and strictly on the prod.

Already the Camas rodeo was living up to its reputation. The bucking horses were real outlaws, and these steers were no ordinary beeves culled by chance out of any herd. They were big, husky brutes, from a wild bunch which had purposely been left to spend most of their time back in the mountains, seldom seeing a man either on foot or horseback. Long-horned—much more so than the better quality beef now found on most of the ranches, including the Diamond—big-horned, ornery.

The rider was after him on the jump, sweeping his horse alongside, leaning over and grabbing the horns expertly, flinging himself out of the saddle and hitting the ground running, twisting with his full weight behind the jump as he went. Scotty watched approvingly. You had to know what you were about on a job like that, to be able to make every movement, every ounce of effort count, otherwise there could be trouble, and plenty of it. Some of the things he'd seen——

Already the riders, one on either side, were dusting their horses up from the sides, ready to haze the big red steer away from the man on foot if anything went wrong, or to be between steer and man after the four-footed actor had been brought to earth, so that he couldn't turn and play a repeat performance. They were getting in on the jump, timing their movements nicely, which helped a lot. A few seconds' delay, sometimes, could spell tragedy.

The steer was fighting hard, with all the brawny weight and strength in a lean, well-conditioned body. But it was soon over. Twisting right, the bulldogger had him down suddenly, sprawling in the dirt, was leaping back and away, the riders were trotting the still bewildered steer over to another chute and out.

Fatty was next, for the Diamond. It was strenuous work for a man of his heft, but weight properly applied helped a lot. This time there was no miscue, as in the calf tying. Fatty got his steer as he wanted him, and as someone remarked then, what chance did a steer have with that incubus hanging on his neck?

Things were going smoothly—too smoothly. There was potential dynamite in the air, and nothing had happened, yet. Several steers had been bulldogged in rather close-to-record time. Off in a corner of the big enclosure, the guards paused for a moment, one of them rolling a quirly, the other fussing with his bandana. There was a momentary respite.

Then, almost without warning, the chute was opening again, and a big roan steer came charging out. Caught unprepared, the bulldogger drove in his spurs and was after him, but that fatal second or so had already placed him under a handicap. Somebody had been careless—either accidentally or deliberately.

Scotty leaned forward, tipping his hat lower over his eyes. He didn't know the rider, but that wasn't necessary. Even if the Curled Quirt brand on the horse hadn't been plainly visible, every Quirt rider wore a yellow bandana to-day to show his colours, just as the Diamond was wearing blue. This fellow was a young chap, tall, lithe, with a tanned face and a determined jaw. He was aiming to get that steer, or else——

His over-eagerness almost cost him his chance. As he swung his horse alongside the plunging steer, already lifting in the stirrups, he leaped, trusting to luck to get a good hold on those rapier-like horns. At the same instant the steer swerved wildly away.

For an instant it looked as though the cowboy would sprawl in the dirt between. Then, somehow, he got his hold, was running alongside the plunging steer. But he didn't have the initial twist of his weight, in leaving the saddle, which can help so much if properly applied, nor had he got the hold he wanted. The steer was dragging him along, his efforts to twist it down futile.

Suddenly, as though enraged by this two-legged creature which hounded it, the steer turned to fight. It was a case now of get it down or be in for trouble, and the puncher was struggling desperately. Scotty half stood up on the fence. Those guards ought to be sweeping in to give him a hand now. It would be a miracle if he ever got the steer down.

But they weren't ready. Caught unprepared, they were somewhere else. For the whole thing was happening fast, as such things do. His face showing white through the tan, sweat-streaked and desperate, the Quirt man was struggling desperately. He bent the arching neck in a powerful wrench, but not enough. The effort, Scotty saw, was costing him dear, and his feet were slipping. And at that moment the steer, instead of going down, was twisting farther around, bringing his head back up in a raking sweep of horns.

One of them, jerked out of the puncher's hands, caught him in the chest, ripping higher, a red streak following it like spilled ink. Then the man was down in the dust, the enraged steer swinging for him again.

It was at that moment that one of the guards tardily arrived, jumped his horse in to shunt it away. Plainly, he had been caught napping, but he was trying hard. Scotty saw that the Quirt colours were tied to his saddle horn and bridle. But he had been too late again.

The next moment horse and rider were sprawling in the dust as well, to the accompaniment of a vengeful bawling from the steer, a high neigh of pain and terror from the horse. Dust rose in a choking, blinding cloud.

The second guard was up now, cool in the crisis; his rope shot out, found those horns now streaming with scarlet, jerked the steer away. Two other riders were jumping out of the chute and to the rescue. And two badly hurt men, both of them Quirt buckaroos, were being carried off the field.

CHAPTER XI

SINFUL SETTING

IT MIGHT all be an accident—but it looked funny, not alone to Scotty, but to a lot of others as well. The Quirt guard, who had been injured along with the bulldogger, had been caught napping, there was no question of that. So, too, apparently, had the second guard, whose cool-headed action saved the day from worse disaster. He was a Diamond man.

But if he had gone into action a few seconds earlier, it might all have been a whole lot different. And who had let the steer out of the chute just at the moment when everyone was unprepared?

These were all questions, and there was no definite answer to a lot of them. But it looked bad. And from the talk going around, it was apt to be bad. Two Quirt men had been hurt. If it had been one Quirt man and one from some other outfit, that would have been different.

For his own part, a lot of things still puzzled Scotty, but the horse wrangler had a strong hunch or so about things. Definitely, they were not what they seemed. Which, on the whole, merely made things that much worse.

Off at the side, Dawn Sullivan was in earnest conversation with Jeff Odom. They seemed oblivious of everyone else, walking slowly, heads bent. Well, naturally Dawn was interested in what happened to the Quirt.

It was none of his business, but Scotty found himself wondering how Odom could bet the Quirt, with a third of it in Dawn's name. Maybe that part of it wasn't involved, but it sounded funny. Again, if she was going to marry him, maybe it was. Scotty climbed slowly down from the fence. It would soon be time for the preliminary rides in the bucking, and he was among the first, according to drawing. He had already bulldogged his steer.

The riding, at least, would give him something to do, take his mind off other things. Or he hoped it would.

He kicked at an inoffensive dandelion savagely. The rides, to-day, would be for fifteen seconds. After that, a man qualified. And on the morrow, a minute would be required of sticking in the saddle. Whereas on the last day, it was stay with a horse till man or beast had won.

Those last were tough rules, with tough horses. Though plenty could happen in fifteen seconds. Jeff Odom was hurrying towards the grandstand now, with no sign of Dawn. So far, Jeff had been an easy winner in whatever he had tried. There was no doubt but that he had ability, plenty of it. And 'most everything else to attract a woman.

Again there was a flash of colour, just a glimpse as someone hurried around a corner of a building and was gone. Scotty felt his pulse quicken a little. He had found his eyes straying towards that same colour combination a dozen times to-day, wherever it might be— in the grandstand, over by the chutes, anywhere around. A green and red checked sort of pattern, big checks, which, though Scotty knew mighty little about women's clothes, he thought was not only distinctive but mighty becoming as well.

Rounding the corner himself, he entered the dusky recesses of the stock room. Several saddles, bridles and other equipment hung on the walls. Quirt equipment on one side of the room, where they had been assigned space, Diamond Head on the opposite, with a few independent riders having stuff on the third wall and bit of floor space. Scotty had wondered about that arrangement. It was on a par with a lot of other funny stuff.

Aside from himself, the room was empty now. Usually there was someone around, but everybody seemed to be outside now. Scotty knew that the Diamond stuff had been brought here from camp and unloaded, not ten minutes before. Since it hadn't been needed up to then, the Old Man had preferred to keep it away from here as long as possible, and Scotty had fully agreed with that choice.

He crossed to his own favourite saddle, almost absently, started to lift it down from the wooden peg, then paused suddenly. The elusive memory of that plaid effect of red and green returned to him like a phantom will-o'-the-wisp. For Dawn must have just come from this room—she must have been the last one in here, the only one since this equipment from the Diamond had been brought in and unloaded.

And in the last few minutes—since it would have been almost impossible until the stuff was brought here—the cinches of his own bucking saddle had been almost cut in two.

Whoever had done the work was no tenderfoot at such a job. It wasn't done in a brash way that would show easy. Not a single strand had been completely severed. None of the cords of the cinch had been cut in a row. Yet each one, somewhere along its length, had been partly cut through, some of them in one place, some in two or three. To the casual glance, the cinches were as good as ever, and they were still strong enough to stand buckling on a horse, to hold while a man swung into the saddle, and to last, perhaps, through an ordinary ride.

But on a fighting, pitching, bucking devil of a bronc— well, it was almost a certainty that neither cinch would last fifteen seconds of that sort of stress. First one cinch would pop ; then the other, its burden doubled, would go as quickly. And almost anything might happen then. Moreover, it could be expected to.

Scotty felt sick. He hated to think such thoughts, but they would not go out from his mind. Who besides Dawn could have had a chance in here? And he had seen something else, while she was walking and talking earnestly with Jeff Odom—something which had hardly registered at the time, but which now had a double significance. The flash of sunlight on something as it was transferred from Odom's hand to her own.

A keen-bladed knife, evidently. A knife with a pearl handle, which he had seen Jeff Odom carrying. Of course, he might be mistaken—he wished he could forget the things he had seen, the logic of the whole affair.

Young Bill Winters came around the corner, whistling, and in at the door. Bill was hoping to be counted as a top-hand pretty soon, though now he found himself doing all sorts of jobs. One thing, he did them well. Scotty turned to him.

" I see you got the stuff here all right, Bill. Nobody got to it while it was in camp, eh ? "

" They sure didn't, Scotty. Things was kept under lock an' key, like the boss said, till I loaded 'em up."

" Anybody here when you come ? "

" Yeh. One of the roustabouts showed me where to put our stuff. He went out then, and I slung it in."

" Anybody else been around ? "

" Just that girl, Miss Sullivan. She stuck her head in to look at something of theirs, just as I went out. Why, anything wrong ? "

Scotty hesitated. He ought to show those cinches to Bill, but he couldn't bring himself to do it. The evidence was too damning—and it might be wrong in the way it pointed. He shook his head.

" I just wanted to make sure that you were keeping

your eyes open, Bill. I figure it'd be a good thing for someone from the Diamond to stick around here all the time, and keep an eye on things. You know plenty can happen. Go on back to camp and get your other load now. I'll stick here and look after things till you get back."

As the kid hurried off Scotty set to work, almost savagely. Taking out cinches and putting new ones in was ordinarily a careful job, but he worked at high speed. There were several extras on hand for emergency, and he had them in before anyone showed up around there again. Then the call came for the bucking, and a couple of the roustabouts hurried in.

" Yuh're up first, Stemple, and yuh've drawn Sinful Setting to start out on. Everybody figgers that even you won't be able to tame that cayuse in fifteen seconds, and a little wrastle now will just get him pepped up right for the finals."

" Sure," Scotty agreed easily. His face gave no indication of his thoughts. Sinful Setting. The cayuse which had never been in a rodeo, but which had killed two men who had tried to ride him, and, as Pop had so graphically put it, darned near got a third. Sinful Setting was owned by the Quirt.

Since fireworks were what the customers paid cash to see, making it the primary purpose of a rodeo, a better horse for the bucking contests could hardly be found. But Scotty knew that it wasn't at all customary to start the opening off with such a cayuse. Horses of that class were almost invariably saved for the finals, for riders who had proven themselves.

Of course, this was the Camas rodeo, and it was supposed to be different—and tough. He smiled wryly. And

F

he was a rider whose reputation marked him as a proved man. But the horses weren't supposed to be picked nor allotted to a man on his reputation, but by lot, in drawing. A Quirt horse like this, for him, at the opening—and after his cinch had been cut that way—well, it was stretching the long arm of coincidence a lot too far.

Sinful was already in the chute, being blindfolded. The two handlers caught up Scotty's big saddle, without stopping to question if it was the one he wanted to use now, and, working from the safety of the chute, slung it on and buckled it in place. Scotty stood by, watching alertly. They hadn't detected anything out of the ordinary, though they might not know what was going on at all. They did a good job under his watchful eye. But nothing more would need to be tried, of course, than what had been planned already.

The three-year-old was a superb specimen of horseflesh. Standing a hand higher than the average cayuse, and weighing nearly a hundred pounds more, Sinful Setting gave the impression of wiriness, of packed dynamite about to explode. He was a light sorrel, with one white spot around the right eye, and no other white mark on him. No more perfect specimen of a hammerhead could be found anywhere.

In the chute, held helpless as he was, he was trying desperately to fight, squealing and trampling in rage. Outlaw and killer was written all over him—renegade in the very stripes which marked his glossy coat. Scars of past battles, attempts to conquer him—with rowelling spurs and shot-loaded quirt. Attempts which had failed, but had added to his hatred for all two-legged creatures.

The announcer was calling them out now—the first event of the bucking contests, the well-known rodeo performer, Scotty Stemple, coming out, la-deez and gentle-men, on—Sinful Setting!

A sudden gasp seemed to break the hush as that last name was called. It needed no build-up to get the effect. As the chute opened, and one of the men jerked the blind-fold off the horse, Scotty could feel that gasp. It had taken everyone by surprise, putting this famed outlaw in for the opening ride. Beyond that he had no time to think of other things.

Bawling his rage, Sinful was out of the chute like an exploding tornado. He came out bucking, stiff-legged, jumping and twisting with all the trained meanness of a thoroughly vicious cayuse which knows his powers, the way to shake a rider, and which disdained to waste a split second in doing it. Those cinches would have been gone by the third jump, on this hell-packed beast.

The cayuse had never been ridden much, but he had had plenty of experience to learn every trick, it seemed, which any bucker knew. Or it may have been just in-stinct with him. As far as time would allow, he was try-ing them all out on Scotty now. Sunfishing, whirling wildly, plunging headlong. A few of the worst tricks of a killer, which take added time, he might still have in reserve, but he was doing his full part towards putting on a show which was bringing the onlookers out of their seats.

For all that, Scotty was remaining in his seat—riding easy, one hand on the reins, the other waving in the air, seeming as much at home as if he had still been perched on the fence and appraising the efforts of others. Any who had doubted, up to that moment, knew that the stories they had heard were true. Scotty Stemple could ride.

He wasn't indulging in anything fancy, for there was no time for that, but he gave the impression that he could do it if he wanted to, even on this twisting piece of wickedness. Then there was a shout from the judge's stand, the guards were spurring in, giving him a chance to slip off as they caught Sinful Setting, proclaiming that he had made his first ride and made it well.

Somebody was probably surprised and disappointed about that, and the gnawing uncertainty as to who that might be completely spoiled the thrill of the victory for Scotty. For he had had to do some of the best riding of his life in that dynamite-filled quarter of a minute, which, because of surprise, carelessness or otherwise, had stretched to more than double that length of time before time was called for him. Somebody had aimed to give those cinches time to break.

He had been the first man ever to stick on Sinful Setting for that long—but the horse was just warmed up to real effort for later events.

Going back to the chute, Scotty watched the saddle pulled off, took it himself and carried it to where Bill Winters was waiting, tossed it on a hook.

"Keep an eye on this till quitting time, Bill—and on the rest of our stuff. Then load it up and put it under lock and key for the night."

He turned at the sound of a dry chuckle from the doorway. Pop was cradling a fresh chew of plug cut in one distended cheek.

CHAPTER XII

MURDER

FOR a moment, the two men stared at each other. Pop's rather watery eyes held a gleam of sardonic amusement, which was replaced after a moment by a look of concern.

"Yuh felt like askin' me what I was stickin' my nose in for, but yuh refrained," he said approvingly. "And that's what I like about yuh, Scotty—among other things. Yuh know how to hold yore tongue, which is a gift I've figgered on cultivatin' these fifty-odd years now, but ain't rightly got the hang of yet. And which there's mighty few that ever do."

Scotty waited. Pop glanced around, fell into step with Scotty as they moved outside. Overhead now, clouds were piling up, shutting away the sun, though the heat still continued to press down like a wet hand.

"Looks like a storm," Pop continued. "And I hate tuh see a hombre like yuh make a fool uh himself, Scotty. Special when there's such matters as good health involved."

"You using a scatter gun to-day, Pop?"

Pop chuckled again, but the sound held no mirth in it.

"Tuh bring down squirrels, eh? Fact is, Scotty, I figger yuh as considerable bigger game 'n a squirrel—and I hate tuh see yuh go over the deep end, account of any woman—'special one that you can't have."

Scotty looked startled.

"I didn't figure I was tippin' my hand that way."

"Likely yuh ain't, tuh most, son. But me, I mebby see a mite more'n some—and I like yuh. That ride yuh made tuhday—it was some ride, if I do say it myself. Now, mind yuh, Scotty, I ain't sayin' a word ag'in her as a girl. She's pretty as a picture, and a nice girl, I guess."

Pop shifted his quid, with the effect of changing mumps from one jaw to another.

"But it stands tuh reason that she's loyal tuh the Quirt ownin' part of it, and tuh the man she's aimin' tuh team double with. And a woman, case like that, can mebby draw the line kind uh crooked and not notice the difference. Sort uh see things through a man's eyes, if yuh get what I mean. And when it comes tuh that, the Quirt sure aims tuh play yuh for a fool—they've got to, after the showin' yuh made on Sinful Settin' tuhday, and with so much staked on this rodeo."

He chewed in thoughtful silence for a minute, sighed.

"Dang it twice! I always like a mite of excitement. Adds flavour, as you might say. But too much is hard on a weak heart. Why, thirty years ago a doc listens tuh my old pump and gives me a kind of a wall-eyed look. ' With that heart uh yourn,' he tells me, ' yuh got to be plumb careful. Any little excitement'll send yuh off, just like that. Be mighty careful. If yuh do, mebby yuh'll last the year out—but not longer '."

Scotty climbed back to his perch on the fence. He was through for the day, for that ride had qualified him for the semi-finals on the morrow. But there were still several rides to be made, and he enjoyed watching them. There were a lot of riders—some with nothing much but enthusiasm and plenty of determination, others with experience and demonstrated ability. Among these were Jeff Odom, who, drawing a tough buckskin, stayed on for his allotted time without much trouble.

Eyes narrowed, Scotty noted that, while a lot of these were tough cayuses, outlaws who had been picked for bucking and who were doing their part beyond any possibility of criticism, none of the other riders, so far, had been given a veteran outlaw such as he had drawn, one which had a reputation like Sinful Setting. The thing looked more and more deliberate. Only—who was handling it all ?

The answer should have been easy, but the more he weighed things in his mind, the less satisfied was he with obvious conclusions. He leaned forward suddenly as the announcer's voice raised again.

" This time, la-deez and gentlemen, Long Jim Jeffries, of the Curling Quirt—coming out on Wickedness ! "

Wickedness ! Scotty leaned forward tensely. There it was again, one of the best riders, from all he had heard, of which the Quirt could boast, next to Jeff Odom himself. And on another thoroughly bad outlaw.

For Wickedness was a veteran of the rodeos from a year or so back. Scotty himself had ridden him the previous year, had stuck with him for the required time— and in doing it had made the hardest ride of his life. Far from being tamed by that ride, Wickedness, before the season ended, had killed a man.

This year, according to report, the big black was meaner than ever. And a Quirt man had drawn such a horse in the preliminaries, just as he, from the Diamond, had drawn Sinful Setting for the opener.

They were out of the chute now, horse and man to-gether. Still together. Whether they would be for long was a question, for Scotty's experienced eye told him that if Long Jim stayed in the saddle, he'd be a rider with an excellent chance of taking top honours at the rodeo.

Yet it was plain, in those first few seconds, that he knew how to ride.

Then it happened, with a suddenness which was somehow appalling. Daylight seemed to blossom, not between rider and saddle, but between horse and saddle. At the same instant the long-threatening storm let loose, a thunder-clap which seemed to shake the earth, a lance of yellow lightning which stunned the eyes, and lashing rain.

Through it Scotty could see what was happening. Confusion had descended everywhere, men were running indiscriminately for shelter. Scotty alone seemed unmoved by the storm, leaning forward, watching. Watching a man being murdered.

For it was plain to his eyes that the cinches on Long Jim's saddle, too, had been tampered with. Yet only the front girth had parted. In the next moment, with Wickedness living up to his name, the saddle had twisted, and the rider, trying desperately to jump free, had somehow been caught. He was down, being trampled under those kicking, flailing hoofs. By the time the guards reached him, a second notch had been carved on the big black cayuse's chart.

And the appalling thing about it was that Wickedness had not killed this second man of his own accord. It had been accidental so far as he was concerned, all due to the planned cunning of some two-legged beast.

While the storm beat and battered at the earth, turning the dusty ground into a lake, Scotty climbed slowly down from his perch, watched them carrying what was left of the last rider away.

"And there, but for the grace of God, goes me," he murmured. "And if there was blood on the moon be-

fore, it'll sure be spillin' over now, looks like. Three
Quirt men the first day—two bad hurt and one killed."

The storm was over with almost as abrupt suddenness as it had begun. For a little while, with supper to
get and the tragic events of that first day to think over,
a hush seemed to hold the town. Then, as evening settled, the air rain-washed and sweet again, the dusk
coming down in mellow splendour from old Diamond
Head and spreading across the valleys, a feeling of rest-
lessness seemed to grip everyone.

The Old Man ate in silence, thoughtfully. He issued
no orders to-night, save for one man to keep a sharp
watch on things, and watched the others straggle off to
the town, with weariness in the back of his eyes. Scotty
went with them. Trouble was in the very air, intangible
as a sense of coming storm, but certain. But there was
no use trying to dodge it when it came. That, too, everyone knew.

" Everybody from the Diamond better stick together
tuh-night," was the only word of warning issued, and
that, Scotty knew, was hard common sense. Not that
he was at all certain that he would follow it himself.

The Bucket of Blood was full to-night—full of men,
which meant that the Quirt was there, making medicine.
And for that matter, every saloon, every building was
full, with the crowds which had swarmed into Camas for
this three-day interval. Faces, both strange and familiar,
were numerous in the Golden Palace as well.

A little speculative hush fell as the Diamond waddies
came in, and it continued more or less wherever they
went. Scotty knew without being told that he could
learn nothing by sticking with them, and there were
several things that he wanted to find out. Unobtrusively

he slipped away, came as quietly into one of the smaller saloons down the street, crowded like the others, but with the crowd which might aptly be classed as neutral— or as close to that as anyone could come here in Camas, where a feud as bitter as death itself was gathering force as had those black clouds of the afternoon.

Hat tipped low, keeping to the shadows, no one recognised him or paid any attention to him. And here was what he had been waiting for—the talk which was going the rounds of the town.

War talk, as he had suspected. The Quirt was bitter. Just how bitter, he didn't quite know—yet. And a neutral corner wasn't the place to find out. He moved on, into the Bucket of Blood itself. There were plenty of strangers here so that he could go among them. Gathered in one corner, with the others and yet apart, the object of hidden but avid attention, were the Quirt men —over a dozen. Scotty edged quietly nearer.

As he did so, Jeff Odom set down his glass and stood up. He rested his knuckles on the table in front of him, staring into the face of his men, and it was evident that he was ready to make some eagerly awaited pronouncement. Silence seemed to fall over the whole saloon, as others realised it as well. But if Odom noticed this, he paid no attention, not even to a lowering of his voice.

" Boys," he said quietly, " you know what happened to-day—but you don't know all of it. Long Jim never had a chance to-day. His cinch was cut—sliced so it couldn't help but break, and then him given a horse like Wickedness. It wasn't an accident—it was murder."

He paused a moment longer after that flat pronouncement, went on.

"There's some other things we don't know for certain yet—and we aren't going to act till we do. But there's one thing that looks pretty suspicious. Our things were in the same room where the Diamond kept their supplies —it won't be that way to-morrow. And in checkin' up, I've found that one man from the Diamond—Scotty Stemple—was all alone in there for mighty close to half an hour!"

CHAPTER XIII

THE BLACK RIDER

SCOTTY smiled wryly to himself. That was putting it plain, all right, so that the word would spread. And over in the Golden Palace the Diamond would be saying things just as blunt about the Quirt. He waited until men began moving around, talking again, then edged unobtrusively towards the door.

His hunch, strong that morning, had grown to a certainty now. There was crooked work going on here, but neither the Diamond Head nor the Curling Quirt was responsible for it, though each firmly believed the other to be back of all the deviltry which had been rolling up like a snowball plunging down a mountain, for long months now.

Such things as that stretched lariat which had spilled his horse—and had turned out to be a Quirt lariat. That was only one of numerous things which had happened, to foster bad feelings between the two big outfits—which both, as it happened, owned the coal that the coming of the railroad would make worth a fortune.

And yet, so far, it wasn't possible to know. For one of the two big outfits *might* be doing it, at that—working cleverly and playing both ends against the middle. Whoever was doing it was clever.

When he had entered the Bucket of Blood someone had been buying a round of drinks for everyone present. That, ordinarily, was nothing out of the ordinary, but to-night, with such a big crowd present, so many of them strangers, it was a bit different, something that would soon run into money.

Now a repeat performance was going on, and Scotty noticed, with suddenly narrowed eyes, that it was the same man standing treat in both cases. Blayley, of the Lazy Azey. He was jovially good-natured, hail-fellow-well-met with everyone. And buying extra drinks just when they would serve to inflame passions already at a dangerous pitch.

Why should one of the small ranchers feel so good as to spend money that way?

Back in the Golden Palace, a few minutes later, he saw that Blayley too had crossed the street, was buying drinks for the Diamond and anyone else who happened to be around, fully as jovial as he had been on the other side. . . .

Fatty Brine, looking worried, joined Scotty. The hefty puncher cast an apprehensive eye over the row of men at the bar, shook his head.

"There'll sure be hell a-popping, Scotty, if they keep on drinkin'. Which won't do nobody any good. If our best men get shot or carved up, we'll lose any chance we

have of winnin' this rodeo—and there ain't anything in
the bets that lets us out on that account."

" So you've thought of that, too ? "

" I ain't so dumb as I look," Fatty said shortly.
" Scotty, yuh tell them to get tuh camp and hit the hay.
Mebby they'll listen to you. And if so, yuh're the only
one they will listen to."

By now the Diamond crew were clustered around the
bar, and Blayley was ordering a second round of drinks.
There was no sign of the Old Man. Scotty slipped
through the crowd, his fingers closed on Blayley's wrist,
engaged in tipping a big bottle to fill more glasses.

" Thanks just the same," he said. " But we're not
havin' any more bug juice to-night, Blayley. There's
riding still to do to-morrow, and it just don't work out
together."

" Why, sure, sure, if that's the way yuh feel about it,"
Blayley agreed readily. " I just wanted tuh help you
boys celebrate a little. The job yuh did tuhday called for
it, seemed like to me."

" Reckon we'd better be getting back to camp,"
Scotty went on. " We can postpone our night life till we
have something to celebrate about."

The others seemed ready enough to accompany him.
Scotty noted, out of the tail of his eye, that Blayley had
lost no time in departing once the drinking was stopped.
He turned to Fatty.

" You go get our horses, cowboy. And bring them
around the corner by the O.K. Café. And watch your
step ! "

Fatty gave him a quick glance, but was gone without
question. Scotty checked the others as they started to
follow.

" Boys," he suggested softly, " there's a plumb fine view of the stars from out the back door here. And I'd like to show it to you."

" I've seen plenty stars before," Sam Purdy demurred. " And I don't like back doors."

" You might see plenty you didn't know was in the lexicon, if you go the front way all together," Scotty said grimly. " I have a hunch the Quirt'll be coming out about the same time, accidental-like—and we don't want to mix now."

" I'm not afraid of the Quirt," another puncher said, rather thickly. " We can clean the whole dirty bunch of them hombres, and the sooner it's done, the better."

Three or four were turning, rebelliously, but they stopped before Scotty's outstretched arm.

" Maybe so," he agreed. " But they're not coming out there looking for trouble, and neither are we. If there's a row to-night we lose the rodeo to-morrow. Let's wait till it's won, then other things can come in their proper place."

" That's sense," agreed Purdy. " Show us them stars, Scotty."

They found Fatty waiting with their horses, swung to saddles. As they started, Scotty glanced back down the street. As he had expected, it was filled between the two saloons now with the departing crew of the Quirt.

Back at camp, Scotty gathered up his blankets and, with only a word to Fatty, edged back towards town again. Camas roared as it had on the previous night, with more enthusiasm than before, if anything. The stars overhead, the same stars which shone down on the silent rangeland, seemed the only tangible link with the life of a cowboy, riding night herd or wrapped in his blanket, with the stars for company. He'd like it a lot better to be out that way to-night, and even the camp was a lot quieter than where he was heading for now.

But Ten Spot, along with some of their other best horses, was in the livery stable to-night, and Scotty's hunch was growing on him. If anything happened to Ten Spot he would be out of a cool thousand dollars, according to the bet he had been led into making. Non-starters to forfeit, and compelled to ride the horses originally entered. Though he wouldn't care for that race on any horse except Ten Spot, in any case.

Also, if Ten Spot and himself were out, that would go a long way to determining that the Diamond would be out of the running, too. Yes, decidedly he had better spend this night and the next where he could keep an eye on his horse.

Going to the back door, he entered the now darkened stable as quietly as it was his custom to do everything. Down in front, a paraffin lamp glowed in the little office. The occasional restless movements of horses, the warm scents and sounds of the stable came plainly. Ten Spot nickered softly as he approached. Scotty sighed a little with relief, rubbed the horse gently between the ears, and, mostly by feel, for the darkness was heavy here, he spread some hay in an empty stall just across the way and put his blankets on it.

He lay for a few minutes, not at all sleepy, staring up into the darkness, trying to figure out the rest of his jig-saw puzzle. A lot depended on it. The control of this whole section of country, for which men, working in secret, were gambling. And beyond property values, men's lives were at stake. One had already been sacrificed to-day on this cold counter of Mammon.

Dozing, Scotty straightened suddenly, tensely alert. Just what had aroused him, he couldn't tell, but somewhere there was an alien sound or presence in the darkness here. And the average person who crept in this darkness wasn't likely to have the same sort of motives which had prompted him to come here.

The hay underneath made no sound as he rose to his feet, standing at the end of the stall next to the long middle hallway of the barn. The sound came again, nearer at hand this time—someone moving stealthily this way—and it was here that Ten Spot was kept.

It was too dark to see more than a vague blur. Scotty waited, then leaped suddenly, had the intruder in his grip.

There was a choked little cry, then the horse wrangler had straightened in amazement, his hold loosening. Even without a word being spoken, he knew whom he held in his arms, and the discovery filled him with mingled emotions. Who he had expected this midnight prowler to be, he could not have said. But he had not expected it to be Dawn Sullivan.

"It's me—Scotty," he said reassuringly, and stood back, releasing her. There was a gasp, whether of relief or not he could not tell, and he was aware of her, very close to him in the gloom, her breath coming a little quicker. Then she was speaking, in almost a whisper, eagerly.

"Scotty! I was looking for you. They told me, over at the camp, that you had come here."

Scotty's arms were still tingling to the feel of her in them, a hunger to reach out and hold her again. He smiled a little grimly in the darkness, his face bleak and strained. He wanted to believe her—but common sense assured him that, as Pop put it, he was being a fool.

"I'm here," he said. "Sorry I frightened you."

"That was all right. I wanted to find you without disturbing anyone, or letting them know that I was here —or that you were. Oh, Scotty, I'm afraid."

He found his doubts of her, as always when she was with him, melting away. There was truth in her voice, and, if he could look into her eyes, now so close that he could almost see the liquid depths of them, he knew that they, too, would be convincing. Her hands were on his coat, impelling.

"What of?" he asked. "If anybody's been bothering——"

"No, no, it isn't that. Not for myself, Scotty. For you. I know why you've come here to-night—to keep watch over your horse, because you're afraid that some-one would try to lame him. You know that something terrible is going on, so I don't need to tell you. But—oh, Scotty, there are more important things than horses!"

He had to steel himself against that drilling quality in her voice. But this was no time to go off the deep end.

"A good horse is pretty hard to beat," he suggested lightly. "But maybe you're right. I don't just understand, though."

"It's you—your life, that I'm talking about, Scotty. Please don't ride again, in the rodeo. Oh, I know how important it all is, that you should, the way things have been shaping up. I don't know who has got them that way, but it's dreadful. Only—Scotty, there are more important things in this world than winning a rodeo, or ranches, or bets. You saved my life—you saved Mart, too. It's a debt we can't ever repay. And I want you to save your own life. Please, Scotty."

G

Even in the darkness, she seemed to read his answer, for suddenly she was clinging to him, and he could feel her slender body racked by sobs. Almost without volition, his arms closed around her, and she snuggled closer to him.

"Of course you won't do it," she said. "But—I wish you would. If they kill you—I'll want to die, too. Please, Scotty, don't ride again."

"I've got to," he said gently. He was himself again, now, as he took his arms away. "And don't worry too much about me. I'm not exactly a tenderfoot when it comes to looking after myself—and I aim to keep in the running."

She drew away a little, as though sensing the change in him, the doubt which had crept back into his mind, even if his tone masked any change in his feelings. Her own voice was a little calmer.

"Well, at least you will be careful, won't you? There is something dreadful going on around here. I don't know just what it is, but it's as though there were another Rider here at the rodeo—like a figure of death, mocking all the rest of us. And it does frighten me dreadfully, Scotty."

"I'll try and be careful," he promised.

"There's another thing," Dawn said. "Mart insists on riding for the Quirt, to-morrow. He's a good rider—but I'm afraid for him, too. You'll—you'll keep your eyes open when he's around, won't you?"

"I sure will," he agreed. "And now—this is no place for you, Dawn. You need to be careful, too."

"Oh, I'm all right," she said a little impatiently. "It's you men who are so stubborn—Well, good night, Scotty —and good luck."

He went with her to the back door, saw her slip out through a narrow crack of it as he opened it. Outside, he noticed, the moon had risen, but for the moment it was partly obscured by a drifting cloud-wrack, so that everything appeared distorted and fantastic, a huge black shadow across the street seemed to take on grotesque proportions. Dawn's own apt simile of a great black rider at the rodeo, with a hooded, fleshless face, came back to him. Involuntarily he shivered a little.

She had crossed where the shadows were deepest, was about to turn the corner of an old shed. And in that moment, from somewhere in the dark pool across the street, red flame bloomed like a night-born plant, followed by the sharp crack of the exploded shell, and he heard Dawn scream like an echo to it.

CHAPTER XIV

SLASHER'S WORK

EVEN his best friends agreed that Scotty Stemple was a cautious man, though on occasion he would walk calmly into the face of danger with his eyes open, as when he had first come to Camas and antagonised Tollard. But it was seldom that he acted wholly on impulse.

Now, however, something stronger, more impelling than anything which he had experienced in his turbulent years on the range seemed yanking him out of that door and across the open, bathed now in full moonglow as the cloud slipped serenely past, until he had reached Dawn.

There was peril in such a course—double peril. For across the street, safely hidden in that black shadow which so resembled a death's-head, was a cold-blooded killer, and Scotty had a strong hunch that the man had fired at this shadowy figure under the conviction that it was Scotty himself who walked there.

Nothing happened, however, as he crossed the open and was in the shadow beyond. White-faced, a little shakily, Dawn was picking herself up again from where she had fallen, and she even managed to laugh a little at the look on Scotty's face as his hands closed on her arms.

" Dawn—Dawn ! " he stammered. " Did he hit you ? "

" It just scared me, I guess," she confessed.

" It was awfully close—" She held up her arm, and, just below the elbow, he saw a red mark on the smooth white flesh—scarcely broken skin where the bullet had passed. At that range, in the deceptive light of moon and cloud-wrack, the killer had almost missed, but that left no doubt of his intention.

" It frightened me, and I tried to run, and tripped," Dawn explained a little breathlessly. " I guess I'm not used to being shot at. But I'm all right, really."

Scotty drew a little breath of relief; then, his first shock of apprehension over, was hustling her quickly on around the corner and to the edge of the street beyond.

Farther down it were crowds, a hum of activity, but apparently no one had heard the shot, or if they had, they were paying no attention to it, figuring it as a chance shot of someone intent on celebrating.

" Where do you live now ? " Scotty asked.

"I'm staying at the Park Hotel, over there. I'll be all right now, Scotty."

"Well, you get there and get inside," he ordered brusquely. "And stay inside at night, while this rodeo is going on."

She paused for a moment, looking up into his face, her eyes very grave as they searched it. Then she had smiled suddenly and was gone.

He watched her cross to where there were other people on the street, then turned back himself, doubling, keeping in the deeper gloom. He might have seen her safely to her lodgings, but there wasn't much danger for her now that the ambush gunman would have discovered that she wasn't his intended target. And Scotty wanted to get back to Ten Spot.

The chances were that, when Dawn had screamed, and the gunman had discovered his mistake, he had travelled for other parts without wasting time. But that was just a chance. Scotty didn't make the mistake of heading for the rear door of the stable again. He found a window, pushed it open, and crawled through. His breath went out in a sigh of relief when he found that Ten Spot was still undisturbed.

Whoever had fired that shot had almost certainly figured that the moving figure was himself. Certainly a dead man couldn't ride in the rodeo, nor one badly wounded. Which meant that no one was merely interested in the amount he had bet on the outcome of the race. Bigger issues were at stake.

Just how big they were, Scotty was beginning to get a pretty good idea, though there was still a lot to this which didn't meet the eye. His mind went back to the crest of Diamond Head, to the outcroppings of coal up

there, the railroad which was coming, and the stretched
rope across the trail, the bullet which had been fired
at himself and Dawn as they rode down the mountain.
There was plenty of trouble here at the rodeo, but even
that, like the men who rode in it, was a pawn in a
bigger game.

And this game, unless something drastic could be
done about it soon, was going to be played on an increasingly bloody board, for ever higher stakes. If
only he knew who was dealing the cards !

Camas, on the second morning of the rodeo, was
busier than ever, if anything. The day was faintly
cloudy, with promise of cooler, better weather for the
events than on the day before. An air of tension ran
like a dark thread through all the gaiety of the celebra-
tion. This was intended to be a time of merrymaking,
of holiday, but there was little of that spirit left now.
More people than himself, Scotty saw, were conscious
of that lurking figure of the black rider, waiting, everyone felt, to ride again before the rodeo was ended.

There had been several fights in town the night before, between adherents of the two outfits, and while
no one had been hurt particularly, feeling even between
those who did not belong to either the Diamond or the
Quirt was swiftly choosing sides, until, save for a few
outsiders who had come here solely in the role of spectators, the neutral element was nearly wiped out.
When the blow-off finally came, it would shake the
whole country.

" And whoever's figuring it, is counting on just that
happenin', " Scotty nodded to himself.

Standings had been posted on a bulletin board, and
whether it was coincidence or not, the Quirt and the

Diamond were practically tied for a number of points
and for the first place in the rodeo, so far. Here again
history was repeating itself.

Scotty was high man, but Jeff Odom was close on
his heels. Third, as Scotty noted with mild surprise,
was Tollard, who had contributed a lot to the standing
of the Diamond.

Tollard was still silent, as he had been ever since
Scotty's arrival at the Diamond, ignoring him and
most of the others of the outfit, but doing his work
and doing it well. Except when he lost that iron control and went berserk, he seemed to be a good man,
but he was still a considerable puzzle to the horse
wrangler. Scotty had been warned that he was like
the elephant, never forgetting, never forgiving. But
like an Indian, Tollard knew how to bide his time.

For the moment, however, he bulked as among the
least of Scotty's worries. The forenoon slipped by,
events being run off smoothly, with two or three old
cow-hands from some of the smaller outfits playing the
part of clowns and seeking to lighten the still-lurking
tension. They received good hands and evoked occasional bursts of laughter, but it was short-lived and
with little of real mirth to it.

The semi-finals in bucking were to finish the day,
and again there was a chance for fireworks. Dawn
Sullivan, Scotty saw, spent most of her time, as on the
day before, in the Quirt section of the stands, and
there was nothing about her appearance to indicate
that she had suffered a bad shock the night before, or
been face to face with death. That news, had it been
known, would have created a greater sensation than
anything else which had taken place. But she had not

mentioned it, apparently, to anyone. She was game, Scotty told himself with a warm glow—game as they came.

Pop, this afternoon, was taking a turn at clowning, and doing it more effectively than any of the others. He could climb on a horse or steer and fall off, contriving to look utterly ridiculous and yet not get hurt, and keep constantly underfoot without getting in the way. There was a pause as the announcer discussed the semifinals in the bucking.

"First up this afternoon will be Jeff Odom, of the Curling Quirt—coming out on Yellow Devil, who threw three men yesterday, all within the fifteen-second interval. Can anyone, even the boss of the Quirt, ride this new outlaw?"

He paused for emphasis. Pop's voice came clearly.

"Sure, he'll do it all right, folks." Pop, riding backward in his own saddle, weaved violently, sprawled across the rump of his cayuse, grabbed its tail, and managed, with a show of much exertion, to pull himself back into the saddle again, clutching the horn firmly with both hands.

"He'll do it, all right. If he don't, I will."

Pop kneed his horse expertly to a chute and out of the way, as the main chute opened and Odom came out on Yellow Devil. It was plain that, set up by his victories of the day before, the outlaw intended to make short work of this would-be rider as well.

He was bad—no doubt of that. But to-day he had caught a tartar. At the end of half a minute of easy riding, Odom took the initiative into his own hands. He quirted the outlaw, spurred viciously. And slipped easily from the saddle after his minute was up, to receive a big hand from the crowd. There was no question but that Jeff Odom could ride.

Just before the ride began Scotty had noticed that Dawn Sullivan left her place in the stands. She was wearing the same red and green plaid outfit as on the day before, one made conspicuous by the fact that it was so different from anything which anyone else wore. In the middle of Jeff Odom's ride Scotty caught another glimpse of it, down near the rooms where the equipment was kept. Just a glimpse.

Purely by chance, his gaze went on back to take in the stands. His eyes came to rest, startled; then he looked again. Dawn was sitting there in her accustomed place.

Save for his narrowing eyes, nothing in Scotty's face betrayed his discovery. But Dawn couldn't be in two places at once, and she was in the stands now. And though that meant even blacker deviltry afoot than he had suspected up to now, Scotty suddenly felt like shouting. A discovery like that was something to shout about.

And something to see about, too. Bill was back at the ranch to-day, relieving some of the other men so that they could come in and get a look at the rodeo. The Diamond shared its equipment room now with several smaller outfits, all of which had been friendly to the big ranch, and had favoured the Old Man in preference to Jeff Odom in the quarrel which was shaking the range. The Quirt had moved its stuff elsewhere.

A man had been left to keep an eye on things. Which was no guarantee that he was doing so, every minute. Some men could have mighty good intentions and turn in a poor job of performing.

The guard was on duty, however, and a swift look around told Scotty that everything was all right in there. He glanced through a dusty, spider-webbed window, saw the room where the Quirt stuff was stored to-day—a room totally empty at the moment.

And the Quirt had three other men coming up for rides this afternoon!

Moreover, they were supposed to have somebody in there, keeping watch. Scotty hesitated. Then, after a quick glance around, he slipped inside the other room. It wouldn't take but a minute to find out—and lives were at stake. Something must be done.

An experienced glance or so told him that the cinches were all right. To bother them took time, and there hadn't been much offered to-day. Also, after yesterday no one was so apt to fool with them to-day. He was just turning away when his eye caught something else.

Scotty lifted it down from the peg where it hung. He had seen this same silver-mounted bridle flashing out there the day before. Phil Devine of the Quirt was inclined towards the fancy in his whole attire, saddle, bridle, chaps, everything. And on the basis of his showing the day before, he certainly had a right to be.

Like every star, he insisted on using his own outfit in every trial. But this one would need a little fixing before it was used again. Done so carefully on the underside of the rein, close up to the bit, that it scarcely showed, the left rein had been cut almost completely through—not from the side, but on the flat surface, so that it would there most readily escape observation.

Scotty turned at a sound. Three Quirt men—Jeff Odom, Phil Devine and another—had entered the room, and, seeing him there with the bridle in his hand, the look on their faces was not reassuring.

CHAPTER XV

MAN KILLER

FOR a moment they stared in silence. Scotty did not make the mistake of trying to drop the bridle or get rid of it, or even to move it, though he knew that the way he was holding it, that cut rein was visible to the three.

Cold rage had replaced the first shock of surprise and anger in Jeff Odom's eyes. Now, with a smooth sureness of speed, his hand moved, came up clutching a forty-five. The muzzle of it looked as big as a cannon as it centred on Scotty.

"So we've caught you at work this time, Stemple." Odom's voice was thick. "Well, this time you've pulled one fast one too many, and I'm going to kill you—shoot you as I would a dog."

The boss of the Quirt was in no mood for any argument.

He had hated Scotty since their first encounter, and it had been gnawing at him like a festering canker ever since then. He intended to shoot now, and as he said, to shoot to kill. With two witnesses to back his story up, of that slashed bridle rein in Scotty's hands, nearly everyone would justify his action—especially after what had happened the day before.

And he didn't intend to wait, to give Scotty a chance to explain or argue. In his mind there could be no explanation of such an act. Already his aim was centring. Scotty felt cold. For once he was utterly helpless to do anything. And then, from the window, came another voice—that of Fatty Brine.

" Drop that hawg-leg, Odom. And don't any of yuh polecats make any miscues, or I'll blow yuh all plumb intuh the middle of next week."

Eyes swung, startled. Levelled in at the window-sill was the barrel of a 10-gauge, sawed-off shotgun. And behind it, the face of Fatty Brine was implacable as doom itself.

For a moment Odom hesitated, his face a twisted fury of emotion. Then, seeing the scattering doom for all of them which lay in a blast from that gun, he obeyed, the revolvers clattered on the floor.

" That's better," Fatty grunted. " I don't know what this is all about—but Scotty can do the talkin'. And what he says goes around here, this time."

Scotty, a little colour returning to suddenly blanched cheeks, hung the bridle back again. His knees felt wobbly, in the reaction from what had seemed certain death. But his voice and his face showed none of it.

" You're mistaken in thinking that I sliced that rein, Odom," he said. " It just happens I didn't."

Odom's laugh was short and disagreeable.

" This time," he said, " you seem to have the best of the argument. But if we catch you strayin' around here again, I'll either kill you or report you to the commissioners."

"Yeh," Fatty sneered. "I reckon yuh'd be right happy about callin' in the commissioners, and tellin' yore story—and havin' us tell ours."

Odom shrugged.

"Let's call it a truce for the present," he suggested. "There's riding to be done."

"Suits me," agreed Scotty. He turned and joined Fatty. Under the circumstances, he couldn't blame Jeff for his suspicions. What the boss of the Quirt didn't yet seem to suspect was that, while there was plenty of deviltry going on, it wasn't the Diamond that was back of it.

Scotty was as convinced in his own mind that the Quirt wasn't back of it, either. That slashed cinch the day before, which had caused the death of Long Jim, riding for the Quirt, this rein on a Quirt bridle to-day —there was plenty of evidence, for a reasonable-minded man, to see that the two outfits were being egged on to battle each other. But it took a dispassionate mind, like his own, which was new to this country and its prejudice, even to argue with them, in their present mood.

Which showed that whoever was doing this was doing a good job of it, and was in a fair way to win whatever victory he sought—unless something tangible could be done pretty soon. He had both the Diamond and the Quirt ready for open battle, once the rodeo was finished, and however it might turn out. Providing the clash could be averted that long.

Fatty grunted as Scotty walked off with him.

"Dang lucky I saw yuh go in there, and then noticed those hombres comin' along," he grunted. "Yuh run too many risks, Scotty."

"You don't know the half of it, Fatty," Scotty said dryly. "But I'm not the only one. I'm right grateful, but—watch your own step, pard."

"Me," said Fatty, "I'm going tuh make a ride pretty soon that'll prob'ly kill me. I ought tuh've known I was out uh my class when I went in for bronc-toppin'. Anyway, if I ever get off, I won't be doing no steppin'. I'll want tuh be settin', and with plenty liniment."

It was like Fatty not to ask questions. His confidence in Scotty, even in the face of such evidence and charges, was unwavering beyond the point of asking questions. And if Scotty wasn't ready to talk, he, Fatty, knew his own limitations and guessed why.

Back on his perch on the fence, Scotty watched again, an indolent-seeming figure that more than one spectator kept stealing glances at. He was counted top-hand at this rodeo, even surpassing Jeff Odom in reputation, and so far he was living up to his reputation. Sitting there, he looked and was becoming more and more of an enigma to the crowd.

Phil Devine was coming out now for the Quirt—coming on Bad Boy. But coming, Scotty was pretty sure, with an outfit that would have been rigidly inspected and so would be intact.

For half a minute he kept his seat, then there was an opening between himself and the saddle, daylight which grew swiftly, and Bad Boy was going on by himself.

Devine picked himself up, plastered with mud from head to foot, where he had struck in a puddle. He limped a little as he turned towards the chute, but waved good-naturedly.

"That soft mud was sure lucky that time," he called, and received a burst of applause for his sportsmanship.

His luck was no worse than that of most of the others to-day. Only a handful were surviving these rough semi-finals. Scotty went out for his own ride of the day, drawing Bad Boy himself. He had inspected his own outfit carefully before seeing it put on, and he made his ride with the same ease with which Jeff Odom had made his earlier in the afternoon.

At least, it looked easy to the spectators. Most of them, who hadn't tried it, had little inkling of the terrific punishment which a rider could take in the space of a minute, on the back of a to-hell-and-back cayuse such as those which were being trotted out here to-day.

Those bone-jarring, stiff-legged jumps, that twisting, snapping motion of sunfishing, turning and whirling in mid-air, which seemed to crack your neck and whole spinal column as a whip is cracked—the buzzing in the ears, rush of blood to nose and ears and mouth, and general punishment—a lot of them were taking plenty to-day, even in the short time they spent riding.

And yet to-day would be nothing as compared to the finals to-morrow. That would be the real man-killer. To-morrow it was ride a horse—if you could—till the horse was tamed down, or you were off. And matched against Jeff Odom and the few others who were surviving to-day's gruelling weeding-out, that would be punishment.

Plenty of punishment. For if two or more of them survived that round of elimination, they would be given fresh horses and kept at it until only one of them was left. The Camas rodeo this year was wild and woolly

—a grudge-fest, spite-test arranged between the Diamond and the Quirt.

They were narrowing down fast. So far, four men had qualified for the finals. Jeff Odom, for the Quirt. Scotty, for the Diamond. Tom McKinstry, riding for Dave Medwick's outfit, the Diamond W; and Turkey Strawn, one of the independents, who had come in solely for the honours and big money offered in the rodeo.

Two others were left. Mart Sullivan and Fatty Brine. If they both made it, each big outfit would have two men in the finals. But it was a big IF.

The kid made a game ride, on one of the toughest cayuses. Give him another year or so, and he'd be up among the best of the bronc-toppers. With five seconds still to go, he was forced to grab leather to keep from going off, and in the semi-finals that disqualified a man, though it didn't matter in the finals, except in the decision of the judges. In event of a tie, they could award the win to a man who in their estimation had made the best ride.

"Concluding the riding for the day, la-deez and gentlemen, and the last of the semi-finals in the bucking contest—Fatty Brine, riding for the Diamond Head, coming out on Sinful Setting!"

Scotty shivered a little at the words, leaned forward more tensely. Fatty was a good rider, despite his awkward-looking build and heft. A mighty good rider, to reach the semi-finals here, with such cayuses as they had been turning loose yesterday. On most broncs he could figure to reach the finals. But on Sinful Setting——

The sorrel, his one white eye rolling, hammerhead lowered, came out of the chute to-day as he had done with Scotty the day before. This was his first warm-up to-day, but he was hot from the opening second. Yesterday he had failed, for almost the first time in his career, to shake his rider at the first bad jump or so, and he was determined to make up for that to-day, to rub out that defeat in a burst of bucking which would show he hadn't really been trying the other time.

But Fatty was riding—riding like a winner. A ragged mutter, which might have been a cheer, went up. Those long, bowed legs seemed to be right now, to curve this cayuse and hang on with, and every trick of the horse seemed to be known in advance by Fatty, who was ready for it. Nearly half of his time had gone by——

Then it was happening. Scotty was the one to sense it first, in the agonised look on Fatty's face. Something was wrong. The next moment he saw what it was. The rear cinch had snapped like a too taut string; the saddle, as Sinful Setting went up in the air, was buckling forward with the horse, sending Fatty pitching over his head—and Fatty's spur had tangled, at the last moment, in the broken, wildly waving cinch.

CHAPTER XVI

DOUBLE CROSS

THINGS were happening fast. The black rider was spurring now, one could almost smell his fiery breath spewing over the field. Fatty was down, the

H

sorrel killer was rearing again, hoofs ready to drum down in crimson death. Neither of the guards could reach him in time.

All eyes were on Fatty and the horse. No one saw the speed with which Scotty's hand had slid into his shirt, or came out again. But they heard the sharp snap of the gun, saw the plunging cayuse rock to the impact of the bullet, stand quivering a moment, and collapse.

Scotty was the first to reach the side of his friend. The cayuse, in falling, had tumbled partly on top of him, and Fatty Brine was limp and bloody. When they dragged him out, it was easy to see that he was bad hurt. He was still alive, but that seemed to be about all. At least one of those vicious hoofs had found its mark.

A doctor was coming up now, and taking charge.

That ended the events of the second day, on a note of tragedy again. Blood for the second day. And this time from the Diamond. Fatty was still alive, but to look at him gave Scotty little assurance that the next day would find him so. And the medico, after his first quick examination, looked about as gloomy.

Scotty turned as a hand on his shoulder jerked him half around, to stare into the inflamed eyes of Jeff Odom. The boss of the Quirt looked as berserk as his outlaw cayuse had done a little while before.

"What's the idea of shooting my horse?" he demanded. "You'll pay for him, blast you——"

Fury blazed for a moment in Scotty's eyes, equalling the flame in Odom's. Then he had control of himself again. If he hit back now, it would be the spark to set off a general war, here in Camas to-night. Which would be playing into the hands of whoever had planned all this deviltry to begin with.

"Wait a minute, Odom," he said. "Let's talk this over reasonable. I had to shoot to save a man's life——"

Odom laughed harshly.

"You were mighty quick to shoot a Quirt horse to save a Diamond man's life! I tell you——"

"I tell you that you're seeing everything in the wrong way," Scotty interrupted. "Can't you see that we're all being made fools of—Quirt men and Diamond alike? We——"

This time Odom's laugh was contemptuous.

"Maybe I was losing my head," he grated. "I aim to beat you and your outfit in the rodeo. Show you up proper. After that's done with, there'll be a settlement of a different kind, and don't you forget it."

He turned on his heel and was gone. Scotty stared after him a moment, shaking his head. It was impossible to argue with a man in that mood, to make him see reason. In fact, it seemed to be impossible ever to find Jeff Odom in a mood when you could talk to him. Even the fact that cinches had been cut on one side as well as the other didn't seem to penetrate to his consciousness.

For Fatty's cinches had been tampered with. How? Despite their efforts, someone had managed it. Scotty shook his head. He saw Carter, standing, crossed over to him. The Old Man looked sick. Fatty had been a favourite with him, and he hated to see a man trampled in any case.

"He's got a broken leg, and is pretty badly bungled up in general," he explained to Scotty. "Doc says he'll know more in a day or so. If he's hurt inside, it'll go hard with him. If he ain't, there's a good chance he'll pull through. Nothin' to do but wait and see, I guess."

That was about as Scotty had feared. By now the scores were being posted for the second day. That, at least, was something to cheer about. The Diamond had forged ahead, in various events, was now well ahead of the Quirt. With an even break the next day, there would be nothing for them to worry about.

Scotty laughed mirthlessly to himself. Nothing to worry about! A win on their part would only increase the bitter feeling in the rival camp, and when things were finally settled, the victor was apt to be as bad off as the vanquished. This thing had gone to the point where it seemed that it must be washed out in blood.

In confirmation, he heard a mutter as he passed along the darkening street. Why hadn't that cayuse done a good job of killing the man from the Diamond while it was about it? Death had come all the way when it was a Quirt man the day before.

That showed how far things had gone, when bystanders, instead of rejoicing that a man's life had been saved, could growl because he hadn't been killed instead.

That feeling was dynamite. And though Scotty had been keeping his eyes open, he hadn't learned much more than he knew the day before. The final blow-off might be postponed another day, for the very reasons which Jeff Odom had given. But if so, and especially if the Diamond won the next day, it would be twice as inevitable, twice as bad when it did break. None of these waddies would be good losers—or good winners.

There should be some way of getting at the truth, of stopping what was coming. But time was growing short, and whoever was backing this was keeping it well under cover. There should be some way to smoke him out—but how?

He had seen plenty that was suspicious. But the only individual to whom it pointed at all was Blayley, and the fact that a man who had a reputation of being friendly with everyone good-naturedly bought drinks for both sides wasn't anything that you could go on.

Scotty turned at a hail. Dawn Sullivan was hurrying up, trying to smile, her face strained and drawn beneath it. She laid one hand impulsively on Scotty's arm.

" I'm terribly sorry, Scotty," she said, " I know that Fatty is your best friend. I'm glad you saved him— glad you killed that Sinful Setting. Oh, it would be better if all these outlaw horses were killed—or just turned out to pasture and this whole thing forgotten."

Scotty nodded. There was comfort in her sympathy, which was real. He knew that now, spoke on sudden impulse.

" I sure appreciate that—and I've misunderstood you some, Dawn. I'm sorry."

" That's all right." Her smile was luminous through a mist of tears. " There's been a lot of that around."

" I hated to kill the horse," Scotty went on quietly. " I always hate to do anything like that. In the rodeos, it's my business to ride the outlaws. But as a horse wrangler, it's my business to keep them from being outlaws in the first place. And any horse that turns bad is just some man's mistake."

He was startled by the look on her face, an expression which he could not quite fathom.

"I think you're right there," Dawn agreed. "Sinful Setting was as gentle as a colt, as promising a horse as I ever saw. He wasn't called that then, but Silver Star." There was a touch of sadness in her eyes. "You see, I used to own him."

She said no more, and Scotty did not question. There was more behind this than he had heard, but it didn't matter much now. She looked up at him.

"I'm going back to the hotel now, Scotty. Maybe I won't see you again before—before you ride to-morrow. I know that you will ride, of course. And I—I'll be praying for you, Scotty. For your safety."

"Thanks." He checked her suddenly, surprised at the huskiness in his own voice. "Maybe it's none of my business, but I'm going to ask you a couple of questions. You can do as you like about answering them. You own a third of the Quirt, I understand ? "

"Yes. I do."

"Is—is your third involved, in that bet that Jeff Odom made ? "

She looked quickly away for a moment; then her eyes met his steadily again.

"Yes."

"Good night." Scotty turned abruptly, a red haze swimming before his eyes. Well, he'd wanted his answer, asked for it, and now he had it. Of course she liked him, was grateful to him for saving her brother, and she was broad-minded and intelligent enough to see that there was more back of this feud than most of them suspected.

But, as Pop had said, she was engaged to be wedded to Jeff Odom. Her fortunes were bound up with his, and that, of course, was where her loyalty lay. He was a fool to think otherwise.

Almost savagely, he turned short into the O.K. Restaurant, slid on to a stool. He didn't care to go back to camp for a bite to eat. The eating house was crowded at this hour, though most of the customers seemed to be out-of-towners who had come in for the rodeo. There was a momentary hush, a sudden tensing of interest as they recognised him. A few hailed him in friendly fashion.

"Mind tradin' stools with me, stranger? There's a few words I'd like tuh say to this Scotty, if yuh'll oblige an old rannyhan."

As the man next to Scotty agreed, Pop climbed up beside him with a sigh.

"Me, I'd ruther squat out in the open and fry my flapjacks, than ride these here high seats," he confessed. "But in this town these days yuh get yore grub where yuh can and need to be dooly thankful for same, I guess. And I've tasted worse cookin' than they do here—even done some of it, sometimes."

He ate in silence a moment, cocked an eye at Scotty.

"What's this I hear about Tollard pullin' out from yore outfit, tuh-night?"

"Don't know." Scotty's mind was elsewhere. "I hadn't heard anything about it."

Pop sawed determinedly through a slice of steak, held it speculatively on his fork for a moment, then deposited it on the edge of his plate again, and sopped at the gravy with a slice of bread.

"When I had all my teeth, I might have downed

that, but it'd been a jaw-wearin' exercise, even then,"
he declared. "Now I know my limitations. Yuh mean
the news ain't reached you, Scotty?"

"What about?"

"I'm talking about Tollard," Pop reminded him
patiently. "I told yuh tuh watch that stray on
trouble's range. Since he didn't get intuh the finals on
the ridin', he's gone as far as he could, garnered himself plenty points in this rodeo, and now he's usin'
them tuh do the most harm."

"What do you mean?" Scotty's attention was centred now. "You say he's quit the Diamond to-
night?"

"That's what I'm tryin' tuh convey, son. Pulled out,
lock, stock an' barrel. Which, just as a side-issue,
means that yuh better watch yore own step. He won't
be above a personal settlement, when he thinks he can
strike from behind, like he's knifed the Old Man."

"How?"

"Yuh ain't got it yet, eh? Well, that ain't tuh be
wondered at none. Accordin' tuh the rules, the points
he's won for the outfit he was ridin' for still belong to
'em. Only, seems he pulled a fast one. Signed independent, but didn't tell Carter nor nobody. Now, when
he quits the outfit official, he takes his points along
with him—and gets away with it."

Scotty saw now. Here was more of this deviltry from
the background. And, cherishing his hate, Tollard had
been able to strike a crushing blow at Scotty and the
Diamond.

"Way it shapes up," Pop went on gently, "instead
uh the Diamond being well ahead, yuh're considerable
behind the Quirt right now. And yuh've got to win

both the finals in the buckin', to-morrow, and the cross-country as well—or yuh're finished."

CHAPTER XVII

THE MAN BEHIND THE BETS

THE news was as true as it was bad. And as was to be expected, it had spread like wildfire around town. Everyone was discussing it now. The Quirt, while they might hate Tollard, were rejoicing at what seemed certain victory now where defeat had loomed as more than a possibility before. There were new bets being made, excited conjecture.

Whoever had planned that move of Tollard's had been plenty smooth, to evade the rules of the rodeo association and still make it stick. But there seemed no question but that it had been done legally. The Old Man had supposed that Tollard was still registered for the Diamond and riding for it, when as a matter of fact he had been registered for himself.

To make it legal, Tollard had written a letter the day before, just prior to the actual opening of the rodeo, enclosing his resignation as a cowpuncher on the Diamond. And here again were earmarks of the whole thing being carefully planned.

Ordinarily the mail would have been brought to camp before noon and the news would have been out. But the letter had been put in with the mail to be

taken out to the ranch that evening, for the men remaining there to look after the work. Just who had
been responsible for this seemed hard to trace.

This evening of the second day, as some of the boys
came in to take their turn watching the rodeo on the
last day, they had brought the letter along with them.
Again timing his movements carefully, Tollard had
walked up to the Old Man not half an hour before the
fateful arrival asking for his pay, expressing surprise
that Carter didn't know all about it. The letter had
arrived as final and legal confirmation at the critical
moment.

There was still more funny business here, in that
Tollard's points had been rated with the Diamond's
for the first couple of days, even though he was registered as an independent. There would, of course, be a
subsequent investigation, and rules passed forbidding
anything of the sort in subsequent years. Which would
make no difference now.

Scotty considered this while he stood on the sidewalk
and picked his teeth. Yellow lights glowed up and
down the street, hitchrails were full of saddled horses,
spring wagons bulked out into the streets. Overhead
the haze of clouds which had tempered the heat all day
was drawing into a solid pall, and there would probably
be more rain during the night.

Most of the stores were still open. His mind made
up, Scotty went to the big general store, and presently
found what he wanted. He stared at it oddly as he
slipped it on one of the fingers of his right hand—a
ring, with a diamond set in it. A good-sized diamond,
which would set him back half of the prize money he
had won in these two days of riding. A glittering stone

which stuck out just like a wart, albeit a decorative wart.

"And me, that's never worn a ring in my life," he mused. "Feels kind of funny on there. Folks will think I'm getting right fancy."

From a feeling of savage repression, the Quirt was in a mood to celebrate now. Out at camp, Scotty knew, would be corresponding gloom on the Diamond side, with Fatty hurt and this latest knife-thrust in the back. Well, it was just the sort of setup he had been looking for. There would be a lot of liquor consumed to-night and tongues, under the added stimulus, would wag freely—he hoped.

The Old Man was keeping the Diamond crew strictly in camp to-night, and probably fuming because he wasn't there. It would be a thankless task to try and look for him in this crowd, and maybe a dangerous one as well, unless they all came along, so probably they wouldn't try it. Scotty, hat pulled low, strolled, keeping to the shadows. With the clouds almost solid overhead now, it was dark enough.

Glancing through the uncurtained windows, he saw that the Quirt was out in full force, all in the Bucket of Blood.

Blayley was there with them, buying more drinks. Just where did he fit in, anyway?

By the time Scotty slipped into the Golden Palace, half an hour later, Blayley was there. And while the Diamond crew were not on hand, there were plenty of their adherents filling the place up, stepping to the bar on Blayley's invitation and taking it straight. Scotty found a secluded table, poured most of his bottle on to an imported palm tree which looked as though it needed a stimulant if it was to last the night out; then, half-empty glass on the table and hat right over his eyes, he was the picture of drunken somnolence.

Unrecognised, no one was paying any attention to him.

There were several men at another table close by, talking among themselves—aiming to do it low-toned, but forgetting with increasing frequency as the liquor loosened their tongues.

"Yuh know, Blayley," one of them was saying, "it st-sth-rikes me as b-blame queer—yuh buyin' dr-dhrinks over here. I t-thought yuh liked the Quirt."

Blayley laughed softly. He seemed as jovial as ever to-night, or a little more so.

"I like the Diamond and the Quirt both, Strawn. Both good outfits, and putting on a good show."

"Yes, it's a good show, all right," another man spoke up. "And maybe it'll be better if yuh feed 'em plenty of the old red-eye, eh, Blayley?"

"Here, you need another drink yourself." Blayley filled the other man's glass brim-full. "You're too sober yet, Rawhide."

"Maybe I am," Rawhide admitted, draining his glass obediently but still with the same mournful air. "But I don't notice *you* getting lit up none. You buy for the other hombres, but yuh ain't drinkin' none."

"There's a time for everything, as the prophet says. A time to be born, a time to die. A time for drinking, and a time for leaving it alone. This is my time for leaving it alone."

"Never did see yuh do much—d-dhrinkin' yoreself, come tuh think of it," Strawn hiccupped. "Allers lettin' the other f-feller do that. But what yuh gettin' out of it ? "

" A lot of enjoyment, my friends. A lot of enjoyment, seeing others enjoy themselves."

" Yuh have a jovial eye, Blayley, but yuh don't give a damn for the rest of us, whether we enjoy ourselves or not—'less it makes a profit for your pants pocket," Rawhide stated, still gloomy. " I ain't kickin' none. But yuh've heard about these bets that Carter and Odom have made, Strawn ? "

" B-bhettin' their ranches agin each other, that t-they'd win this—thish rodeo ? "

" Have another drink, Rawhide," Blayley urged, and he seemed a bit uneasy.

Rawhide obediently drained his glass again, coughing a little, but without apparent effect.

" We're all friends here, Blayley," he protested. " It ain't any secret, is it, that they didn't bet their ranches against each other ? "

" Who the devil w-would they bet with, then ? " Strawn demanded owlishly.

" That'd be tellin', and mebby Blayley wouldn't want that. Would yuh, Blayley ? "

" Better have another drink, Rawhide."

" Sure. I'll have as many as you say. But it won't get me drunk, Blayley. Ain't nothin' can affect me any more. There ain't even any taste to this bug-juice. Oh, I'm sober, and the more I drink the more sober I get. I won't be sayin' anything yuh don't want told."

Strawn slumped over the table now; his glass rolled and crashed on the floor. Blayley stood up, and Rawhide followed his example mournfully. A minute later they had gone outside.

Scotty waited a full ten minutes before he moved, his mind busy. Here was more news of a startling character. He had supposed, as had practically everyone who had heard anything about it, that the two big ranch owners had bet their outfits, each against the other. Since they did have cash bets with each other on the outcome, that had seemed a reasonable supposition.

But either because they had not been proud enough of their folly to brag about it, or had considered it nobody's business, the truth had remained hidden. If Blayley and Rawhide were right—and it looked as though that might readily be the case—then the whole setup was radically different from what he had supposed.

Rawhide believed that Blayley held those bets. If he was right, then Blayley was the man behind all this deviltry. Posing as a good-natured, jovial friend to all, he was playing both sides against each other. If they came to open warfare and wiped each other out, that would still fit in with his plans.

There was Tollard. Quitting the Diamond at this eleventh hour, taking his points away from them to try and cripple them. Tollard was evidently getting paid for what he was doing. It would take more than brains such as he had to plan such a thing and execute it the way it had been done.

Cut saddle girths, bridle reins, and other general meanness, directed against both outfits—with everything planned to make each ranch believe that the other was responsible.

And the payoff! Both bets were not merely that they would win the rodeo—which either outfit might do in

number of points—but that they would beat the other!
And it was being planned that both of them should
lose, one way or the other. In which case both big
ranches, with the rich vein of coal and all the rest,
would be forfeit!

It was some scheme, all right—if it could be worked!
And the devil of it was that he couldn't go to either
Carter or Odom and tell them about the coal, warn
them of the plot. Odom wouldn't listen for a minute.
And to tell Carter, in his present mood, would just
mean a blow-up and war to-night—which would be
playing directly into the hands of the man who was
hoping for that to happen.

CHAPTER XVIII

MIDNIGHT MARAUDER

THE livery stable was dark again, but Ten Spot
nickered softly as Scotty came up, and that was a
relief. The big near-pinto was in good shape for the
next day, and if he could be kept so—for Scotty had a
hunch there was trouble in the offing here as well—
it would make a big difference when the finals were all
totalled up.

That was the queer thing about this gambling. It
was all illogical, as Scotty knew, but if he didn't make
that ride, he'd fork over what he had bet, and if the
others lost they'd pay their bets and feel they were

doing the right thing. A debt of honour, in a trans-
action where that ingredient was mostly conspicuous by
its absence.

Well, human nature was a queer thing, when you
considered it in the other fellow. Or in yourself, for
that matter. Scotty had done plenty of things in the
last couple of weeks which had surprised himself, and
it looked like the end was not yet.

Spreading his blankets, Scotty went to sleep. The
distant noise of the still wide-awake town didn't bother
him. And he wasn't fearful in his mind of what might
happen here. The same trick which had been used
against him, tying a rope across the trail, could work
pretty nice here, he figured. Only this time it was a
couple of strings across the hallway of the stable, the
ends running to his wrist.

He woke, conscious of a sharp jerk on his wrist, in-
stantly alert. The blackness seemed to be absolute now,
and there was the steady beat of rain on the roof high
overhead, the monotonous drip, drip of the eaves. Even
the habitual lamp in the office at the far end of the
hall was out now, proof that the hour was late. All
sounds from the town had ended, as the rain settled
down and dampened spirits.

In a stall nearby a horse moved restlessly, proof that
some intruder was near. Scotty stood up, ears strained
to catch a sound. The intruder might not have noticed
kicking against the string at all, or the feel of it might
have warned him that something was not exactly as
it ought to be.

The silence was almost too perfect, save for the
breathing of horses in some of the other stalls. And
meanwhile the intruder might be slipping into Ten

Spot's stall, ready to get in his work. Guiding himself by a hand on the rough side of the wall, so that he would go straight, Scotty crept forward.

There was plenty of danger in this sort of thing. If he could speak to Ten Spot, he could blunder against him in the darkness, crawl under him or whatever he wanted to do and be perfectly safe. But with some intruder about Ten Spot would sense that, too, would be high-strung and tense, and if he found somebody around him he might lash out swiftly with both hind hoofs.

That was a chance which the intruder would have to take, and Scotty as well. And the midnight visitor, whoever he was, was likely to have a knife. To blunder into him in this pit of blackness was nothing very pleasant to think about.

Folks could talk of wild gunplay here in the west, of heroes who thought nothing of danger, but that, as Scotty knew, was plain bunk. A man didn't fool with death if he could avoid it, any more in one section of the world than in another, and the flesh could shrink from contact with a ripping, gouging knife, or a searing, killing slug of lead, with your imagination working overtime. Besides, Scotty was a cautious man.

It was evident by now that his visitor, whoever he was, was on guard and smelling trouble. Otherwise he would probably have used a light, to avoid too much risk from the horses in other stalls. Only a fool, or a man aware of danger, would do it any other way.

"And he's not a fool," Scotty reflected. "Let's hope I'm not either."

For what he was about to do might come close to that, if he did it wrong.

I

Ducking down behind the boards of a stall, he held one hand just above the level of it and scratched a match. A match was taboo in a barn such as this, but he could manage it all right. If he could discover what he wanted to know by using it, without stopping a bullet, he would be all right.

Those boards were pretty good protection—unless the other man happened to be on the wrong side of them. In which case he'd be worse off than ever.

Almost as he scratched the match and the flame ballooned up, he had it out with a flick of the wrist, then he was jumping towards a sound in the hallway. Jumping, maybe, to encounter a gun or a knife. His hands closed around something, and at the feel of that rough, plaid-like fabric, for a moment he was almost unnerved.

He had felt that same fabric in his arms the night before. Then in the next instant he knew that, whatever this intruder might wear, it wasn't Dawn he held in his arms to-night, but a man—tough, wiry, fighting like a wildcat. But fighting, praises be, with a gun in one hand, which he hadn't quite had time to use. Scotty much preferred that it be a gun to a knife blade.

For a minute there in the tense darkness they struggled almost on even terms. The other man was trying desperately to tip that gunbarrel up so that it would be lined right if he squeezed the trigger. Scotty was trying just as hard to prevent him from bringing it into play.

They staggered back, struck the edge of a stall, and a sharp pain shot through Scotty's side where the rough board bruised his flesh. Quick to sense what had happened, his opponent was trying to repeat the trick. Teeth clenched, writhing a little, Scotty yielded to his pull away, but as the backward slam began he twisted, powerful muscles cording, and he heard the dizzy grunt of his opponent as he struck that sharp end of the stall board in turn.

It had accomplished one purpose. His enemy had dropped his gun in the shock of it, and now they were fighting on more even terms. Scotty had had a feeling that if he could come to grips with this deadly unknown he would be able to tell who it was. But in that almost absolute blackness he could tell nothing definite, except that he had tangled with about as tough a customer as he had ever known.

By now one thing was apparent. The other man was finding that he had a bigger job on his hands than he had bargained for, and he wanted to get away before something went wrong. Twisting like an eel, almost as slippery as that boneless fish, he might accomplish his purpose. And if he got clean away in the night, that would be a victory.

Scotty let go with one hand, judging as closely as he could, struck hard with doubled fist. He knew by the feel that he had hit just about where he wanted to, on one cheek. Knew too, by the grunt of pain and the way that wart-like diamond turned the ring on his finger as he struck, that he had driven it deep into the flesh. There would be a cut there which would show for several days to come.

Almost at the same instant something like an exploding stick of dynamite seemed to hit him. Vaguely Scotty realised that the other man, rendered desperate, had taken advantage of his moment off guard, following that blow, to bring up a knee to his solar plexus, to jar him with a fist at the same instant. Writhing, half dazed, Scotty staggered back.

For a minute he leaned there against the wall, gasping for breath. He heard the retreating sound of the other man's footsteps running down the hall, heard the back door open a little and close again, but he was helpless to follow. Had his opponent realised how badly that foul blow had crippled him for the moment he would probably have stayed to finish the job he had come for, and Scotty along with it.

But he hadn't known that. His breath back, Scotty spoke reassuringly to Ten Spot, felt around in the darkness until his fingers encountered the dropped gun. But in the light of another match there was nothing about it to give him a clue as to the owner.

It was an old, well-handled Colt's .45, but a hundred almost identical guns could be found in Camas to-night. The diamond on his ring, however, showed scarlet.

Thoughtfully, since it had served its purpose, Scotty slipped the ring off, wrapped it in paper and tucked it safely in a vest pocket. If he was thinking of getting married, now, that stone could be transferred to a lady's ring, and it would be a right nice one.

Scotty sighed. Since he wasn't thinking of any such thing, he'd just take it back, after things had quieted down around town, and get back what money he could for it, telling the clerk he'd changed his mind. He'd likely be out about ten bucks for the rental, but if that mark showed up on a cheek to-morrow, as he figured it would, it would be worth the price.

Meanwhile, no one had seen him wearing the ring, Which might or might not be worth something,

Scotty moved to the rear door, slid it softly open. The rain had almost stopped, the clouds were breaking to a rich yellow hue, like distant gold, as the moon struggled to break through. There was water standing on the ground, plenty of it, plenty of mud underfoot. Which would be a bad factor in the finals of the bucking, and doubly bad in the cross-country race to-morrow. From being merely a man- and horse-killing race, it would become a nightmare.

Here were tracks in the mud, as he had expected. But already they were so rain-filled that it was impossible to tell much about them. Or to follow them any farther than the nearest board sidewalk.

Well, since he'd had that hunch about the ring, had been so lucky in working it, that didn't much matter. He could go back to sleep without much danger of being disturbed for the rest of the night. Unless he figured it wrong, somebody would prefer to take a chance on stopping Ten Spot in the race to fooling around this stable any more in the dark.

He was just sinking off to sleep again when he started up suddenly, with an idea that turned him cold. Then, grimly, hurrying as fast as possible, he was drawing on his boots, the grim knowledge in his mind that he'd get no more sleep to-night. But if this last hunch was right, too—then sleep was a minor matter. He was running as he left the stable.

CHAPTER XIX

PROWLERS OF DARKNESS

FOR this midnight intruder, while obviously a man, had been dressed in woman's clothes! He had felt the tweed cloth under his hands and that, coupled with what had happened the day before, was another proof that whoever was doing this was trying to hide behind a petticoat. More especially, it was an effort to make him believe that Dawn was doing this sort of thing.

Dawn had come here to the stable the night before to see him. And that, perhaps, had given this midnight prowler the idea. But whoever it was, he was a cold-blooded proposition, and he, or they, might not stop here. To try and throw him off the scent something might be done to Dawn, to-night.

It seemed like a far-fetched idea, Scotty realised, but he was dealing with a strange personality. That was becoming more and more apparent. That glimpse of a dress the day before—which was a copy of what Dawn had been wearing—had been intended to convince any-one that Dawn had been prowling around the Diamond storeroom. He'd feel better if he knew that Dawn was all right. His hunches had been working out too well lately.

There was a dank chill to the air at this hour, following the rain. An obscure star or so blinked in watery fashion from breaks in the clouds; it was wet and unpleasant underfoot. Then, as he struck a board sidewalk on the main street, his footsteps made a hollow sound on the soaked planks. The dark, silent buildings seemed devoid of life, a world removed from the bustle and

gaiety which had streamed through the streets a few
short hours before.

The Park Hotel was on a side street, off from Main
—a two-story, frame affair, as dark now and silent as
the rest of the town. Seeing it so quiet and aloof, some
of his fears left him. Then, as he skirted one side of it,
the moon broke through the clouds and here, along
the side, were fresh tracks in the mud—tracks into
which water was still seeping.

They led to a kitchen window and ended there. The
window stood open. Without hesitation Scotty climbed
through, saw the imprint of wet boots leading to a back
stairs, and followed. He had reached the head of the
stairs and was peering around, for now the tracks no
longer showed, the gloom was thicker here. Then
there came a smothered cry from somewhere down the
hall.

With dim sounds of conflict to guide him, Scotty
reached a door, flung it open, and was inside. Here the
light from the window, opposite the climbing moon,
was scarcely a lightening of the pall, but he could see
a confused, struggling heap on the bed, and he jumped
for it.

The intruder had heard him, however, and was a
shade the quicker. Scotty's clutching fingers closed on
a mass of bedclothes, the window was being jerked up
and, by the time he could reach it, the visitor had
dropped, was already gone in the night.

"Scotty!"

The horse wrangler turned at something in Dawn's
voice. She was sitting there in bed, her hair dishevelled,
cheeks flushed, staring at him, incredulous joy in her
eyes. Despite the dimness he could see that, could

sense the relief and welcome in her voice. He turned
towards her, something choking in his throat.

"Dawn! Are you hurt?"

"No." She shivered a little. "That—whoever it was
—had just come in. I woke up, and tried to scream,
but I was muffled in the bedclothes, and I—I tried to
fight. I was terribly frightened. And then you came."

"You poor kid." Scotty's voice held an unaccus-
tomed tenderness. "This feud is sure being hard on
you—and it's a mighty low sort who'll drag a woman
into a man's scrap."

Something glittered beside the bed, there on the
rough board floor. Scotty stooped, picked it up. It was
a small pen-knife, with one blade open. Dawn stared at
it with widening eyes as he examined it.

"Scotty—what was that for?"

"Have you ever seen it before?" he asked.

She shook her head.

"No. But I—I can't understand."

"He wasn't going to hurt you—much," Scotty said
grimly. "He just aimed to put his brand on you, like
I put mine on him a while earlier this evening."

"What do you mean?"

"Somebody came in the livery stable to-night. And
aimed, I figure, to hurt Ten Spot so that he couldn't
run in the cross-country to-morrow. Just a knife-
thrust in the fetlock to lame him would have been
plenty. And whoever came was dressed like a woman,
in tweeds like you've been wearing—and getting the
idea, I figure, from your having come to see me last
night."

Astonished incredulity was in her eyes now.

"I still don't understand, Scotty."

"There's been a lot of underhanded work going on since the rodeo started, and I've seen some of it. There was an attempt made yesterday to try and make it look like *you* sneaked into the supply room of the Diamond and slashed the cinch which pretty near got poor old Fatty killed. I saw the flash of a dress which looked just like yours—but you were in the stands right then."

He shook his head and smiled at her, but the smile was as strained as her own face.

"Don't ask me why—I've been trying to figure it out, but I don't know—yet. I only know that that's the way it shapes up. This hombre in the stable to-night must have figured that he could still fool me— and make the Diamond hate the Quirt that much more. I cut his cheek—and he thought that if you showed up to-morrow with a cut cheek it would at least help to throw me off his track."

They were talking in lowered tones, Scotty sitting on the edge of the bed. Suddenly he coloured a little, stood up.

"I—I reckon I'd better be going now. I had a hunch he might try that, so I came and sort of tracked him right to your room. I don't think you'll be disturbed again to-night, and I—I ain't just in the habit of busting into ladies' bedrooms thisaway."

Her hand, warm and vital, came up to clasp his, to pull him back to his seat again. Dawn's smile was warm, with something in it which warned him anew that he'd much better be going. But his legs were strangely lax.

"You don't need any excuse, Scotty, not after the way you've saved me. And this isn't the first time.

Oh, Scotty, I don't know how I can ever thank you for all that you've done—for me, and for Mart."

"Shucks, I don't need any more thanks." Scotty was stammering now. "You've given me more'n enough already."

Dawn was eyeing him now with almost pleased delight, an imp of mischief dancing in her eyes.

"Scotty, I believe you're embarrassed! Why, this is about the first time that I've ever seen that impenetrable calm of yours shaken! You know, it's nice to discover that you're not exactly a man of iron, but are human like the rest of us."

"Human!" Scotty repeated. "Dawn, if you only knew——"

He stopped himself, drew back. Next thing he would be making a fool of himself. There was a lot of difference between gratitude and—and what he was fool enough to keep thinking about. He stood up.

"I'm human enough that I'll need to get some sleep, if I'm going to be in good shape for the rest of the programme to-morrow," he said. "And, while you're plumb beautiful already, still far be it from me to rob you of your beauty sleep. Considerin' what it's done for you already, that'd be a crime."

Dawn flushed a little, her eyes starry.

"And he can make pretty speeches, too," she said, but something in her tone belied the lightness of her words. "Some time, when you don't need to get your sleep, you must make more of them. And if you will be so kind as to toss me that robe over the back of that chair there, and turn your back for just a moment——"

Scotty obeyed, his fingers fumbling a little with the softness of the thing, conscious suddenly that there was

about it that same faint, elusive perfume which seemed
to accompany Dawn wherever she went.

Just what it was he couldn't have said. It was rather
intangible, like the suggested fragrance of wood violets,
and somehow reminded him of them, cool, remote,
fresh, on a hot, troubled day all around. Little patches
of sunshine dappling the shade, a tiny, cold stream,
with mossy rocks and wild strawberries growing close
by.

And a moment later she was beside him at the door,
her hand in his, speaking in a whisper, though the hotel
still seemed to sleep, undisturbed by what had happened. This was the hour when sleep was the heaviest of
the night, when it was a real effort to rouse the average
sleeper.

"I'm going to let you out the door, like the honest
man you are," Dawn said. "When I have a caller I
can at least do that much for him."

Scotty would have preferred that she let him find his
way out alone, though he was loath to say good night.
He was silent, and she felt his arm rigid under the light
touch of her fingers as she led the way down the stairs
and to the door.

Here, once she had drawn the bolts softly, was a tiny
porch, with the moonglow, now supreme in the heavens,
beating softly down upon it. Dawn looked up at him
and, at something in her face, Scotty's iron will became
fluid. The next instant she was in his arms, her lips
against his own, cool and soft and sweet. And he
realised, with a kind of dazed incredulity, that her
white arms, remarkably soft for all their strength, had
crept up about his neck, that she was returning his
kisses.

For the next few moments such mundane affairs as sleep and rodeos and impending disaster were forgotten. This was more than he had dared hope for, even to dream of, and though he couldn't understand it, he was willing to accept the miracle of it now without asking questions.

Then there was the sound of a step at the edge of the porch and they broke apart, turning to stare in surprise at the man who stood there, eyeing them from under lowered brows.

Jeff Odom was handsome. There was no doubt of that. Handsome as the devil. And in that moment it seemed an apt simile. For his face was distorted with rage, his lips drawn back from snarling teeth. For a moment he stared at them, and then he contrived to smile—it might have been a leer—and words broke from him thickly.

"So this is your midnight visitor, Dawn ? " he said. " I might have guessed it—if I wasn't such a blind fool. I couldn't sleep, and I looked out of my window from the Palace across the street and saw somebody dropping out of what I thought was your window. Or I thought I saw somebody drop out. The light must have been playing tricks with my eyes. So I dressed and came out to investigate."

He was silent a moment, while neither Scotty nor Dawn could seem to find words before the seething fury, the cold scorn in his tone. Then he spoke again.

"My mistake, of course. One I'll not be making again. I suppose by rights I should offer my apologies, eh, for interrupting this—lovers' meeting? Even if I did crash in with the best of intentions. And so,

good night. As for you, Stemple—I'll settle with you
—to-morrow."

That last choked threat was rather an anticlimax to
the rest, but Scotty knew that it was driven out of him
by a rage which he could not down. As he turned,
Dawn seemed suddenly to come to life again.

"Jeff," she panted. "Oh, Jeff, you're wrong. You
don't understand. Jeff——"

But Jeff Odom, hard and bitter, was gone.

v

CHAPTER XX

HELL ON HOOFS

AS SCOTTY had expected, there was no more sleep
for him that night. He had too much to think
about—and it was too hard to keep his mind on practical things. But they had to be figured out.

That story of Jeff Odom's, explaining how he had
come to be there—it all sounded logical enough. Yet
somehow it seemed odd that a man should wake up at
that hour, and glance out at that particular moment,
and figure what particular room something was happening in, in a dark building across the street. And
then, if he was alarmed enough about danger to Dawn
to investigate, to stop and dress so fully and carefully.
But maybe he was telling the truth, at that.

Fatty Brine, the next morning, was no better. The
medico shook a grave head and reported that by all the
rules of the game, Fatty should be dead by now. And

it was better than even money that the black rider would catch up with him yet, before this bout was finished.

His face set and grim, following that report, Scotty went about his business that morning with a sharp glance for the face of every man he met. Though it was highly probable that whoever had a cut cheek would be careful to keep out of his way to-day.

Feeling out at camp was worse than it had been the day before. Just as it was in town. There was an un-declared truce between the two big outfits until the rodeo itself was over, while each sought to surpass the other. But after that, win, lose or draw, they both figured to settle some matters by direct action.

The thought wasn't encouraging. This sore had fes-tered too long, here in the shadow of Diamond Head. If trouble once did start, it would be a bloody battle while it lasted. And Scotty knew from experience that once such hot-headed struggles were finished, that was usually only the real beginning of trouble. Cold, cal-culated killings would follow in its wake, a long-smouldering and deadly feud which made a hell-hole out of a once prosperous, peaceful range. He didn't want that to happen here.

Out at the rodeo grounds things were in readiness. A few last-minute events were run off to clean the slate, to which the crowd paid scant attention. Then the finals in the bucking were to begin. To-day the four survivors would be pitted against one another and against the worst cayuses to be found. Except for Sin-ful Setting, who would kill no more men.

Turkey Strawn was first on Yellow Devil. The only independent rider to reach the finals was putting up a game battle to cop top honours, and for a few minutes it looked as though he would conquer the horse. Then, with the suddenness which usually marks such things, he seemed to lose control and hit the ground a moment later. One out.

McKinstry, riding for the Diamond W, was up next, and down almost as quickly. Wickedness lived up to his name, much to the chagrin of the W rider who, being a Diamond man, had aimed to show that a Diamond W was as good as a Diamond Head when it came to bronc topping. But these the crowd still regarded merely as preliminaries. The real contest which they had been waiting to see would be between Jeff Odom and Scotty Stemple, and they had known it all along.

Opinion was pretty evenly divided. Jeff Odom was a local man, but the feud which had reft the range for the last half decade prevented opinion swinging solidly behind him as such. And Scotty, in his days of riding here, had won admiration for the performances he had turned in.

The question now was, which of these two riders was the better? And could either of them stay with the outlaw cayuses that were still on the waiting list? Such horses, it seemed, just couldn't be ridden—not for long.

Jeff Odom was up first. Attention centred as the announcer spoke :

" Jeff Odom, riding for the Curling Quirt—coming out on Wickedness ! "

Scotty, perched as usual on the top bar of the fence, shook his head. That was bad medicine, to send him out on such a cayuse. The outlaw had earned his name and, after just throwing one rider, and doing it with so little effort, he would be twice as much on the prod

as usual. If Odom rode him, he'd be doing a grand job
—and a job that was man-killing.

The fact that Scotty had ridden the big black the
required time the year before meant nothing. That
had been a ride for the conventional length of time, and
had done nothing towards taming the cayuse. As his
killing of two men since then, including Long Jim,
afforded ample proof of.

Jeff Odom's face was set and tense to-day, compared
with his usual easy attitude of confidence. He was
still seething with rage, was glad of the chance to take
it out on the horse. Almost at the start he spurred
savagely. And if he had wanted results, Scotty saw
grimly that he was getting them.

Wickedness went up into the air in a trick which
Scotty remembered—a devastating whirl and buck in
the middle of the air, calculated to shake a man loose,
almost to spin the flesh from his bones. He came down,
stiff-legged, with Jeff Odom still in the saddle. A ragged cheer went up from the crowd, even from adherents
of the Diamond Head. That was riding.

It was. But it had shaken Odom. Scotty could see
that, and he sympathised with him. Right about now
he probably felt as though his spine had been driven
up into his head, and then the whole thing broken in-
dividually and collectively.

But Wickedness wasn't giving him much time to
think.

He was rearing now, standing almost straight up on
hind legs. That was a killer's trick as well, and Odom
was trying to bring him out of it, flailing savagely at
the hammerhead with doubled quirt. But this time the
horse was determined to go through with it. A sigh

went up from the crowd as the big black went crashing down.

To escape such a devastating act was something that couldn't be done more than one time in ten, even by the best of riders. You had to kick your feet free of the stirrups and jump at the right moment, but that was only a beginning. It was almost impossible to judge the time, or to figure where the falling, writhing body of a horse coming down in such a manner would catch you. Even if you guessed right the chances of getting clear were pretty slim. If you guessed wrong, made a single error—then the chances were all against your ever making another.

But Jeff Odom had made it. He was on his feet, still clinging to the bridle reins, as the big black cayuse sprawled, then, shaken a little himself by that trick, was scrambling back on his feet.

This time a whole-hearted cheer went up as the boss of the Quirt jumped and was back in the saddle as his horse regained his feet. For a moment the black stood unmoving, seeming to shiver a little. Scotty saw that there was a smear of blood on Odom's face.

Then, far from conquered, Wickedness was plunging again—bucking, sunfishing, plunging clear across the field in a series of hops which would shake a man up worse than nearly anything else. But his spirit was flagging now as he tried to get results.

This rider was different from any he had ever fought it out with before—the second man who hadn't been shaken off, no matter what he tried. He had been sure, the year before, that he could shake that other rider, given time. And just now another man had quit him without sticking very long.

But this rider wasn't quitting. He was spurring again, lashing with the quirt. And presently it was the horse who quit, his days as a rodeo terror ended. Yet Scotty saw that the man had taken just about as much punishment as the horse.

He hoped soberly that he could do as well. No man could do better, he was certain of that. Whatever else he was, Jeff Odom was a bronc-topper.

It was Scotty's turn now. Wickedness had been led away, a horse that anybody could ride now, and who would probably end his days as just another cow pony. But there were plenty of others who were far from conquered.

Scotty inspected his outfit grimly, detail by detail, watched the horse saddled, swung into the saddle as the blindfold was jerked off and the chute opened. Scotty Stemple coming out on Unknown.

The bay cayuse might have been unknown a few weeks before, since this at Camas was his first rodeo experience. He had been a wild horse up to those few weeks ago, and was at least four years old, a hater of bits, saddles and spurs, and above all, of the men who wielded such things.

But he was already known as one of the worst outlaws who had been rounded up for this Camas show. He had been out twice in the preliminaries, twice in the semi-finals, and all four men who so far had tried to ride him had hit the dust after his first two or three jumps, and hit it hard.

Scotty gained some idea why in the first few jumps. Unknown had a gait of his own, a peculiar twisting quality to his bucking that was decidedly disconcerting. Only once before had Scotty topped so individual a horse, and that had been an experience—though not a pleasant one. This, he saw, was going to be another.

For a couple of minutes, circling the enclosure, Unknown bucked around it steadily, with little variation. An older, more experienced outlaw would have changed pace sooner, but Scotty had a grim conviction that this was about as tough as anything could be, kept up persistently. He was dizzy, with a taste of blood in his mouth, a drumming in his ears, his whole body wracked and pounded. Then, suddenly, the bay cayuse stopped, standing stock still.

Scotty waited, tensely alert for the next move, glad of the respite. A cold, calculating eye rolled up at him, but for a full minute, while he considered, Unknown made no motion. Then, with a quivering of flesh as though about to explode, he started suddenly, breaking into a dead run at a bewildering speed, heading straight for the fence. And Scotty knew enough about outlaws to know that he didn't intend to swerve.

Just what Unknown's thoughts may have been the bronc-topper didn't know. Whatever peril of bruises there might be for him he seemed willing to risk if in doing so he could smash the two-legged creature on his back, as a fly is crushed between a hand and a wall. And unless he could turn him, Scotty knew that was just what would happen.

To try and stop him was out of the question. Almost as fast as the cayuse, Scotty leaned forward suddenly until he could grab one bridle rein almost up at the bit. Then, with all the strength of arms and shoulders, he pulled—a sudden tearing jerk that swung the horse around despite himself, swerving him from the fence with a scant half-dozen feet to spare.

Narrowly saving himself from falling headlong, Unknown straightened. Then he leaped to the goad of spurs, the slash of a quirt. But now it was Scotty who was deciding what should be done, was driving him to do it—racing around and around again, until he brought him to a sudden halt with savage reins. And this time Unknown was quite content to stand, dancing a little, but his fight all gone. A second outlaw had been tamed.

Scotty swung rather wearily to the ground. It had been good riding, all right—not quite so spectacular, perhaps, as that the boss of the Quirt had been called on to do, but just as hard, taking just as much out of a man. A day's ordinary work in the saddle was not so hard a grind as that.

His mouth felt dry, but there was still the taste of blood in it. The crowd was wild, yelling for another deciding ride between them. But Dave Medwick, sitting in the judge's stand with shrewdly narrowed eyes, saw what most of the crowd had failed to guess.

It was good stuff for a rodeo crowd, of course—mighty good. And highly spectacular. But you could kill a man this way, and there was still the cross-country. He beckoned to the two of them.

"You boys have made mighty good rides," he suggested. "I doubt there's a bronc-topper alive could beat you, and mighty few to equal you. But there's the cross-country coming up—and it can easy be the deciding point. How about calling this a draw and letting that settle it?"

Scotty waited, watchful but silent. If Jeff Odom wanted to agree, it would suit him fine. He had a lot of respect for Odom's ability, and no desire to try and

best him at some more of the same. It wasn't worth
it. But it wasn't for him to say.

He didn't need to. Odom still looked a little sick
from the punishment he had taken in that ride, but his
vengefulness was at least equalled by his gameness—
as well, perhaps, as by his damfoolishness.

"The rules call for ridin' till there's a winner," he
growled. "And I'll see any bronc-topper from the Diamond in hell first 'fore I'll split honours with him."

"Me, in especial?" Scotty asked.

"Yeh, you special," Odom snarled. "Bring out another cayuse, and I'll ride it for yuh."

CHAPTER XXI

KILLER CAYUSE

JEFF ODOM coming out on Yellow Devil! This time
Scotty seemed as sleepy-looking as ever as he sat
there on the fence and watched, but he was more intent
than usual. Whether the boss of the Quirt realised it
or not, he had taken a lot of hard usage during the
first ride, following two days of punishment, and it
wouldn't take much to tip the scales.

Yellow Devil was intent on tipping them. And the
sooner the better, so far as he was concerned. He was
heartily sick and tired of the whole affair, anxious to
somehow get back on the open range where he could
snuff the air and run free as a king again, and getting

this over with should help. And while some of these other cayuses might fail to shake their riders, he had no fears on his own account.

He started with a trick not often thought of, but devastating when done properly—and there was nothing lacking in his execution of it. Bucking steadily, he was spinning around, making the turn in as short an area as it could possibly be compassed, around and around. A thing to shake a rider to pieces and to make his head whirl. It was then a question whether the man could outlast the cayuse—or turn him.

Scotty, watching, saw that the horse was master here, at least for the moment. Jeff Odom was trying desperately, jerking on the off-rein, to straighten him out of that frenzied circling but, head down, teeth clamped hard on the bit, Yellow Devil seemed to realise that he had the other fellow going, and he was keeping right at it.

In desperation, Odom tried a desperate expedient. Reversing his own tactics, he jerked still harder on the other rein, catching the cayuse by surprise, sending him stumbling to his knees.

A moment later the horse was up again, but Jeff Odom was on the ground. That last pitch had been too much.

Sprawling there, sick and reeling, he was in no position to get to his feet and do anything, and the guards were too far away, caught unprepared for the moment. Only Scotty, who had been looking for trouble, was ready.

A handful of spectators saw him half rise to his feet on the corral fence, saw a loop in his hand shoot out swift and true, settle around the neck of Yellow Devil as, ears laid back, mouth agape, he swung and started back for the man rolling on the ground.

Scotty took a swift half-hitch of his rope around the top bar, and then the horse was sprawling, neck jerked around, a few feet from where Odom was getting unsteadily to his feet.

Scotty loosened his rope a little as the guards came sweeping up and climbed down. Jeff Odom looked at him queerly as he walked off the field. The boss of the Quirt had failed by a fraction to make his ride. But since he had tried it, it was up to Scotty to try in turn. Only by beating Odom's last ride could he come up winner.

He had drawn, he saw, a horse which was pretty well unknown, though on a couple of occasions it had done some vicious bucking. Fleabite had a ragged, rangy look, but he was long and powerful. He might be easy to ride, but evidently the judges didn't figure him that way. Nor did Scotty, as he watched Fleabite being saddled.

But the opening was disappointing. Fleabite did not come bawling out of the chute. He walked out of it like an old cow horse, paused for a look around, and turned his head to regard Scotty curiously, even impersonally. Then, without an instant's warning, he charged for the fence, intent on whirling against it and brushing this incubus off.

Scotty let him go. It was dangerous, mighty dangerous work on an outlaw bucker, but he judged which way Fleabite was aiming to go, jerked one leg out of the stirrup and flattened himself on top of the saddle. The horse, whirling, hit the fence hard, bringing a grunt out of him. As he veered away again, Scotty had both feet in the stirrups, while a sudden awed cheer went up from the crowd.

Fleabite had had enough of that trick. It had hurt him a lot more than it had the man, and without profit. He settled down to some straight bucking, slowed as though tired and stopped. It looked as if he were through.

Most of the crowd thought so. But Scotty was doubly alert. This wall-eyed cayuse had tried that trick before, and he might have something more in mind. A moment later, with the same suddenness as he had shown before, he tried it.

This time it was an attempt to lie down and roll over. Ordinarily an easy thing to check, his sudden change from an apparently defeated cayuse to one about new deviltry was disconcerting. Scotty half sensed what was coming. He kicked his feet loose, jumped free. As he hit the ground, he jerked suddenly on the bridle reins, lashed out at the horse with his quirt. Surprised again, Fleabite forgot his idea of trying to roll, which might have loosened the saddle, and Scotty had to ride him until he was through. As Fleabite came up, Scotty was in the saddle again.

This time he assumed the aggressive, spurring hard, slapping the cayuse with his hat. For a minute or so the big horse responded, but there was little spirit left in him. Already he knew that he had been outsmarted and mastered. Two of the worst tricks to be sprung during the rodeo hadn't worked. A minute later Scotty rode him to the chute and out.

Pop strolled up, his jaws working mechanically, grinning a little. Nothing seemed to impair his joviality.

" Kinda takin' chances, wasn't yuh, Scotty ? " he

asked. "Flippin' that lariat rope thataway. Mebby it'd ought tuh won the fancy ropin' prize for yuh, but that Fleabite hoss come right close tuh spillin' yore bacon, way it looked tuh me."

"Close enough," Scotty agreed. "But I aim to ride in the cross-country, and it'd seem sort of lonesome without Jeff Odom in it."

"Well, every man tuh his taste, they say. Some even likes these here little olives. They's a lot of men from the Diamond wouldn't have been flingin' that rope, even if they'd been perched where the chance was good. And I misdoubt that Jeff'll appreciate it much."

In that he seemed a good guesser. Jeff Odom was as surly as ever, seeming more bitter, if anything, that it had been Scotty Stemple of the Diamond who had saved his life. Well, that was all right with Scotty. He hadn't done it for Odom, particularly, nor in the line of expecting thanks. He'd have tried the same for any man, and it had been luck that he was perched in a place where his rope would reach.

At that, he was disappointed in Jeff Odom. The man had possibilities—a lot of them. But he was too arrogant, with too surly a disposition. Get over that and he might amount to something. The shadow of a grin creased Scotty's mouth. Maybe he hadn't done much to make the Quirt man love him, at that. Figuring up their meetings, and the way they'd been at cross-purposes every time, there might be something to the idea.

He'd started in by licking Jeff Odom the first time they met, and that was something pretty hard to swallow. Last night, Odom had seen Dawn in his arms, and this time he'd been the man to save Odom, when he was too far gone to get up and run. Yes, those things could be mighty galling to a man with red hair.

The standings had been posted, and Scotty viewed them with mild surprise. It seemed that things had a habit of running this way every year. First the Diamond had been well ahead. Then Tollard had pulled out with his points, and that had put the Quirt into what looked like almost a safe lead. But now, with him winning the finals in the bucking, the Diamond had pulled up again so that the two outfits were neck and neck—not only that, they were exactly even.

Which meant that whoever beat the other man in the cross-country would win the rodeo for his outfit. Neither of them needed to finish first. But one would come in ahead of the other, and that would be the deciding point.

Unless—and the idea caused Scotty to stop suddenly and stare unseeingly ahead for a long minute. There was a first, second and third in the cross-country, and there were about a dozen horses entered for the race. Just suppose that neither he nor Jeff Odom, who were the only contestants from their outfits, should finish among the first three?

It didn't loom as very likely, on the face of it. They had been the outstanding performers at the rodeo to date. But then, likely things weren't happening, not at this rodeo. Whoever was back of this plot was doing a lot of figuring, and a lot besides mere figuring. With so much at stake now, it was only common sense to assume that he'd keep right on along the same lines, harder than ever.

In points, no other man or outfit could catch the

Quirt or the Diamond, even if they won the cross-country. Which, the way it had worked so far, didn't matter. For if neither of them won any more points now, they would be tied for first, as in some previous years—but neither would be the winner.

And, under the terms of those bets which had been laid, with neither one winning nor beating the other, whoever held the bets would simply take over both ranches!

Yes, the whole thing was decidedly on a par with what had gone before. Funny that other folks couldn't see what was happening here, but it seemed like they couldn't. Everybody figured that it was merely a scrap between the two ranches. A tie would make both of them that much more ready for a big fight, even if they didn't have a thing left to fight for.

The figures might have been juggled somewhere, or that tie might be an accident. There wasn't anything to be done about that now. It could be done only with the Quirt and the Diamond demanding an investigation, working together. Which was out of the question.

So far, he'd seen nobody with a cut cheek. Scotty settled his hat a little tighter. It looked as though he'd really have to do some riding to-day. Too bad Fatty wasn't around to watch things, as he'd done the other day.

But if he could hold things even a little longer——

Even as the thought came to him there sounded the sudden blast of six-guns in a pounding fusillade.

CHAPTER XXII

MYSTERY BULLETS

SCOTTY turned and ran. He didn't like that sound, didn't like it at all. The way smokeless powder was being burned, it had all the earmarks of the blow-off which he had been fearing. And to try and do anything now was probably like working to put out a prairie fire with a match. Still, sometimes a match could start a backfire——

Only an empty street met his eyes as he rounded a corner. The smell of burned powder seemed still to hang on the air, like the faint scent of coming storm. But there was no one in sight, either standing or lying in a pool of blood.

From the shelter of a building Scotty considered it with narrowed eyes. There was something funny here —mighty funny. Too much on a par with all the rest that had been happening lately. Some celebrant might fire off a shot or two, but not that many—and not without attracting attention. Everybody was staying severely away from here. Scotty didn't care to risk stepping out in sight, either. There might be more lead filling the air.

What he wanted to do now was to get back to camp and ask the Old Man a few questions. Maybe he should have done it before.

"Be nice to have brains and know just how to use them," he grunted. "But a hombre can't have everything, I s'pose."

Carter was smoking a big cigar and sitting on the tongue of the cook waggon, his eyes fixed on the distant sprawling bulk of Diamond Head. He looked older than when Scotty had come to the ranch, with new lines around his eyes, but he roused and smiled as the horse wrangler came up.

"That was a pair of mighty fine rides you made, Scotty," he said. "Mighty fine, suh. I was aiming to tell you so, but seemed like I lost you before I had a chance. The way it looks now, we're still in the running."

"Seems we are," Scotty agreed. "And I figure that gives me the right to ask a few questions."

"Gives you the right to ask any in the catalogue, son. Reckon the Diamond would be gone already if it wasn't for you."

"About this bet, now. The way I've been hearing it, you stand to lose the outfit, ranch and all, if we don't win?"

The Old Man blinked and coughed, as though the smoke had choked him. Then he nodded.

"That's about the way it shapes up, Scotty. I got hot-headed, sort of, I reckon. Mebby made sort of a fool of myself. And now I have to leave it to you to pull my chestnuts out of the fire."

"How'd you come to make such a bet? Odom have anything to do with it?"

"Well, he sort of got under my skin, I'll have to admit. Has kind of a way of doing that."

"But who holds this bet? It isn't Odom."

Carter's gaze jerked suddenly away from the mountain.

"Why, hell, of course it's Odom," he exploded. "Who else would it be?"

"Seems like I'm misinformed, then. I heard it was somebody else."

"Oh, that?" The Old Man waved his cigar, scattering ashes with the gesture.

He went on: "Sure, it was another individual who consummated the deal, so to speak. But acting for Odom, of course."

"In that case, how come that the Curling Quirt is bet on the same terms? Do *you* hold that bet—or a third party, actin' for you?"

"Me? Great Jehosaphat, what are you talking about, Scotty? The Quirt can't be bet on those same terms——"

"Happens it is. And do you have any inkling why somebody else is stirring up all this hell broth between the two outfits, tryin' to aim that neither one wins— so that he gets both of them, if they don't?"

The idea, plainly, was a new one to Carter. He stared a moment, shook his head.

"It can't be, son. Just can't be. If there's such a deal, it's done by Jeff Odom to throw dust in our eyes. Things go that way on this range."

"Any idea why somebody's so anxious to get the outfits?" Scotty persisted.

"Why, sure, the Diamond's worth plenty. When you can catch an old codger like me off guard, and make out to steal his chestnuts, a fox would hide his head in shame if he didn't do it."

"There's more than that to it. The railroad's building towards this country."

"Sure, sure. It'll help out some—raise the price of land a bit, maybe, make it easier to ship stock out and supplies in. But it's nothing to get excited about."

"Maybe not, but figured along with that big vein of fine coal, up on top of Diamond Head, it might be.

That coal's about half on Diamond territory, half on Quirt."

"Coal?" Carter tossed his cigar away, stared. "Scotty, you ain't by any chance sort of inferrin' that I'm just a plain damned fool, are you? Or trying to pull my leg? Coal? Seems like there's a lot of things going on around here that give me the brand of ignorance."

"I'm just explainin' a few of the things making up the picture," Scotty said patiently. "The coal is there, all right, for I've seen it. Now what like was this hombre that holds the bet on the Diamond? And he'd likely have a name to go by."

The Old Man frowned a little, his mind again jerked away from a tempting new bone just as it was trying to sink teeth into it.

"Him? Calls himself Denton, I remember. Wears black whiskers and has straps on his pants, sort of like Uncle Sam. Horned in when Odom and me was having that little argument, and first thing I knew, darned if I hadn't made that fool bet."

"You haven't seen him around since?"

"Don't believe I have, now you mention it. Said he'd be out of town for a few days, but would aim to be back by the last day of the rodeo. Which is to-day."

"He bet you something in turn, I expect?"

"Cash." Carter snorted. "Not a quarter what it should have been, though. And if he loses, likely he won't show up again at all. They say there's no fool like an old fool."

Disappointed, Scotty hoisted himself off his haunches. He was getting nowhere fast, the way it looked.

"Guess I'll take Ten Spot and go into town again," he said. "Sort of be ready for things."

Carter stood up also.

"Don't you take this thing too hard, son. Me, I've made a fool of myself before and lived through it. There's things worth more than land and cattle. Some son-of-a-gun must have tipped this Denton off that I was hot-headed. Only way I resemble Jeff Odom that I know of, and I'm ashamed of it. But we'll make out, anyway."

Scotty wasn't fooled. There was a huskiness in the Old Man's throat which he couldn't keep out, and he was still blinking, though the smoke had cleared away. This prospect of losing the Diamond was hitting him hard. He wasn't young enough to start over again. And that hombre Denton, who had been so careful to keep out of sight—he might be a stranger, but whoever he was acting for was no stranger. That hot-headed weakness for gambling, which was a common failing of both big ranch owners, had been well-known and cannily seized upon.

"Speakin' of your horse," Carter was saying. "I sent Bill Winters into town with Ten Spot a little spell back, to find you. Had him go to the livery stable and bring him here, and give him a nice rubdown. Ten Spot looks all set to ramble. Likely you'll find him waitin' at the rodeo grounds."

But there was no sign of Bill or Ten Spot around there. The grandstand and most of the place was practically deserted now, and would remain so until time for the start of the cross-country that afternoon. The other events had all been run off; there was an intermission of a few hours in between.

His uneasiness increasing, Scotty looked around. Of course, not finding him there, Bill might have taken

the horse back to camp, or over to the stable again,
or be looking for him around town. But with so much
dependent on things to-day, he wanted to know where
Ten Spot was.

Again there was a sudden flurry of gun-fire. The
thing was getting funny, but he'd look into it. This
time the sound had come from a side street, a place
where things were ordinarily pretty quiet, blocks away
from the centre of the town, which roared and seethed
again. Once more the firing had died away just as
quickly as it had begun. Scotty came to the place and
slowed.

It had all the look of a repeat performance—save for
one thing. Not a man was visible either up or down
the street. Any stray citizens had probably ducked
prudently for cover when the fireworks began, and none
were left, either in vertical or horizontal position. But
Ten Spot was there.

A slow spot of colour glowed in Scotty's cheeks as he
approached. Ten Spot was tied to a hitchrail, and
there was mute evidence to be read.

The horse was dancing and quivering with terror,
for he had always hated gun-fire. Some horses never
could be trained to take it. He hadn't been touched,
that Scotty could see, by any of those bullets. Which
was either luck or mighty poor shooting, or both. For
there was evidence that, though the bullets had evidently been fired from an alley across and down the
street, Ten Spot had been the target.

Just beyond the horse was an old rickety shed, apparently long unused. Weeds grew rank beside it, an
old sign was askew and so badly faded that nothing
could be read. Bullets, fresh bullets, had peppered the

L

shed on both sides of Ten Spot and above him, almost cutting the pattern of a horse themselves. Those shots had been close.

Whoever had done it had evidently wanted to make it sound like a gun-scrap between two opposing groups, had intended to kill Ten Spot in the doing, so that it would be put down as an accident. Something, perhaps Scotty's approach, had scared the gunman or crew away before that purpose had been worked.

"Not lookin' for a dead man, was you, Stemple?"

CHAPTER XXIII

COW COUNTRY CLASSIC

BLAYLEY stood there, teetering a little on the balls of his feet, watching Scotty with a half-smile that was somehow disconcerting. His jovial good humour seemed undimmed, despite his question.

"You got one?" Scotty asked.

"Well, not exactly," Blayley sighed. "But then again, it's all in the way yuh look at it, likely. There's one here I figgered yuh might be int'rested in havin' a look at. Just down the alley and back in a shed."

Scotty followed him, tensely alert. Down where those other bullets had come from, which had peppered so close to Ten Spot. Here was another old shed, unused like the one where the lead had mostly found its mark. Blayley pushed open a sagging door, indicated with a nod of his head the figure sprawled on the dirt floor, crimson spreading in a patch of the ancient dust to make a little red puddle of mud.

For a moment Scotty felt his stomach contract. It wasn't necessary to look closer to recognise Bill Winters, or to know that he was dead.

" What happened ? " he asked.

Blayley was still smiling. It had the air of a smirk which, once mechanically planted there, would not come off. And it had nothing to do, Scotty guessed, with the real humour of the man. He had worn it like a mask until it had become one.

" I was comin' along here when I heard them gunshots start. Naturally, I was interested. Been sort of expectin' trouble, though I've hated the thought of it startin'. I looked down this way, and I was right surprised to see that Winters, here, was the only hombre in sight—and him shootin' at your horse, there, tryin' to keep out of sight when he done it. Your cayuse, he was fightin' the reins and dancin' pretty skittish, which, along with me happenin' by, was likely all that saved him from gettin' shot—accidental-like."

Scotty's lips were tight.

" What else ? "

" I was kind of astonished, Winters being a Diamond waddie himself. Not that he give me much time tuh think about it. He saw me, and swung his gun my way and started to blastin'. Seems like that's the way a guilty conscience works." Blayley sighed and shook his head. " Lucky for me he was such a durn poor shot. I didn't have no choice but to pull my own hog-leg, and I don't often miss."

Scotty stooped, turned Bill Winters partly over with

a hand on the shoulder. Winters' gun, empty, lay beside him in the dirt. And on his right cheek was a small, deep, nearly round cut—such a cut as might have been made with a gouging pen-knife, or from a diamond.

"I found somebody and sent him for the sheriff," Blayley explained. "He ought to be here any time now. Here he comes."

The sheriff and the messenger hurried up. Blayley repeated his story, and the sheriff nodded.

"Lucky yuh shot straight, Blayley," he commented. "Though I'd never have figured it of Bill Winters. Which goes to show that yuh never can tell." He turned to Scotty.

"If I was you, I'd kind of watch my step. Seems like there's a lot of trouble around here lately, and it's so danged mixed up, it's right difficult to tell where it starts in or leaves off. Though maybe this'll finish it, so far's traitors in yore own outfit's concerned."

It was good advice, all right. With a creepy feeling raising the short hairs of his scalp, Scotty untied Ten Spot and swung into the saddle. With the sheriff standing there now, there wasn't apt to be another "accidental" bullet fired from some alley right now. But he was willing to bet long odds that there would be one, or several, before the race was over with.

And the devil of it was that there wasn't much of anything he could do about it—except to go ahead and be a target. That cross-country had to be run.

He'd had good luck so far—a lot more than any reasonable man had a right to expect. Except for being beaten up by the whole crew of Quirt men, along with Fatty, he'd escaped with a whole skin up to this point.

It would be almost too much to hope that he could keep on that way.

Bill Winters' luck had run out, for one. There was a lot about that that Scotty didn't like at all—but for the moment it, like some other things, must wait a while.

Back at camp, he told Carter what had happened, and left orders that Ten Spot was to be watched every minute until he came for him again. Then he turned back into town. He'd get a bite to eat at the OK Café and, incidentally, he'd keep his eyes open. He had found that cut cheek which he'd been looking for, but that was a long way from solving things, even if he had been hopeful. There was still that whiskered hombre who was either back of it all or acting for whoever was—and who held the bets.

Scotty slid on to a vacant stool and was promptly served, though the café was rushed at this hour. But the man who had ridden the buckers to a finish, who had pulled the Diamond Head out of a hole and brought it even again, was about the most important personage in Camas to-day, and none of the other customers demurred at this favouritism.

He accepted it without interest. Here, where he was surrounded by a crowd, things were safe enough. Come the race, and out pretty much alone, things could be different. He finished, tossed a silver dollar on the bar, strolled outside. It was about time to be getting ready.

The stands were filling fast again when he reached the grounds on Ten Spot. The race would begin and end here, compassing a big swing in the meantime. Other riders were coming up, ready for this classic of the cow country.

Here there were no rules, no restrictions, either for horse or rider, save that the horse must be a regular cow pony, and carry a regular stock saddle and bridle. Weight of horses, equipment or riders was entirely up to the rider.

And these horses and men gathered here lived up to those specifications. Someone announced to the crowd that there were a dozen entrants.

Jeff Odom was riding Lightning for the Curling Quirt; Scotty Stemple on Ten Spot for the Diamond Head; Tom McKinstry for the Anchor; Turkey Strawn on Firefly, independent; Si Denton on Midnight, indepen——

Scotty turned to look as the name hit him. Si Denton. There couldn't be any question of it. The man was tall, with long, black hair and long black whiskers. Otherwise he had the look of a cowboy and he sat that big horse easily, though it was pitching and plunging, impatient with the delay.

So that was the man who had the bets on the two biggest ranches in the country, who had kept so carefully out of sight up to now. There was no chance to talk to him, with the horses already lining up. He aimed to be in this ride—but Scotty had a hunch that he wasn't here for the purpose of trying to win the race.

And he was riding a black horse—a powerful, snorting creature who looked able to go the distance. A rider on a black horse——

Scotty shook his head. He was letting his imagination get the best of him. He looked around. Eleven horses here now. Where was the other? Then the announcer called it out as it came trotting up.

"Mart Sullivan, riding independent to-day, on Nameless."

Scotty gave the kid a smile. A moment later, as if by chance, Mart was beside him. Looking straight ahead, he spoke out of one corner of his mouth.

"I'm in this tuh kind of side you, Scotty—you've got one friend along."

Scotty's heart warmed. There was a lot of comfort in that idea, whatever good it might or might not do. Another horse pushed up, crowding them apart. Denton, he saw, was keeping well away from him, by accident or intention. There was no sign of Tollard. He had figured on seeing him here—and the fact that he wasn't did not lend reassurance.

From the stands, he saw Dawn stand up, wave to him, returned the gesture. Then she was waving to Jeff Odom, but, stony-faced, the boss of the Quirt pretended not to notice. Scotty eyed him sharply. Jeff Odom looked bad now. He had been pretty badly used up in the bucking that morning. Scotty knew how he felt. If he lasted this race out, starting it in that shape, he would be lucky.

And to-day, in this final event, the black rider— maybe not the man on the black horse, but the rider who had already struck him twice since the rodeo started—would be riding with the rest of them, gunning not alone for Scotty Stemple, but for Jeff Odom. Only you couldn't tell him that.

Swearing, the starters had them lined up. A gunshot roared in signal, then they were away, plunging in eagerness to outdistance all the other cayuses heading along with them. Two or three riders were already out in front, over-eager. Scotty preferred to stick with the crowd as long as he could, and he saw that Jeff Odom was prudently doing the same. So, too, was Denton.

The first mile was given to a thinning out process, a few horses getting ahead, others falling behind. Nothing much would happen near the start, of course. It was too close to town. That first mile was easy going, too —save for one thing. Soft ground.

The heavy rain of the night before had left it spongy, muddy in places. Which made it doubly hard for the horses. It would be, more than ever, a killing race. Scotty was holding Ten Spot in, keeping the eager horse to an easy gallop. Those fools who were well ahead wouldn't be in at the finish at all. No horse could keep such a pace over this course.

Jeff Odom was a little ahead of him. Otherwise they were almost alone for the moment, with hills ahead and behind shutting off sight of the others. And now, abruptly, from somewhere in those same hills, a rifle cracked, the bullet, aimed to kill, barely missing its intention.

But it was not an entire miss. Scotty felt the shock of it as it struck his left arm, a little below the shoulder, the searing agony as it ploughed through flesh and out again, missing the bone. The shock of it almost knocked him out of the saddle.

CHAPTER XXIV

GUN-BARREL GLEAM

JEFF ODOM'S head jerked around sharply. For a moment he stared, first from Scotty to the spot where the shot had come from. But already they were past where they could see back to where the gunman crouched in ambush.

Ten Spot had seemed to leap forward at the sound of the gun-fire and, without looking back, Scotty knew that the killer had been at least a quarter of a mile away, and that it would be useless to try and find him. Everything was in his favour for escape. Besides, to try and hunt him down now would be doing exactly what he wanted, and lose all chance of winning the race.

Ten Spot and Lightning were almost neck and neck now. Odom turned to Scotty, his face set and very puzzled.

"Whoever fired that shot, Stemple, it wasn't a Quirt man," he jerked out. "Though why the devil should they be shooting at you—man, you're hit!"

Scotty nodded. The first tearing agony of the bullet was over with, but it still hurt plenty, and was bleeding a lot. It had been a clean wound, from a steel-jacketed bullet, high-power, but that didn't keep it from being bad.

A few inches farther in, as it had been aimed, it would have reached his heart cleanly. It took good shooting, at a man on a running horse, to come so close at that long range.

"Get off," Odom ordered harshly. His face was a

study in mixed emotions, but he was already pulling his horse to a stop. " I'll tie it up for you."

" No need to—waste time with me," Scotty gasped, wincing with pain as he brought Ten Spot to a halt as well.

" You can't ride with it that way," Jeff Odom ground out. " Though I suppose you'll ride if it kills you." There was grudging admiration in his tone. He was on the ground, whipping out a white handerchief, jerking off the bandana about his neck, which was the Quirt's colours in the rodeo. " We'll tie it up and still have plenty of time in this race."

He ripped the shirt sleeve away with his knife, stared at the wound a moment, teeth set, then went expertly to work, tying the wound with another strip drawn tight above it to check the bleeding as much as possible.

" Why the devil should anybody shoot at you ? " he rasped out angrily again. " I tell you the Quirt doesn't do such things."

" It's not the Quirt or the Diamond that's back of all this deviltry, Odom," Scotty said steadily. " There's a third party holdin' the bets on both ranches—and if neither you nor me come in among the first three, we're in a tie. Ever figure that out, and what it means ? "

Odom's fingers stopped for a moment, and he stared with sudden comprehension. Three or four other riders were sweeping past, with curious glances towards them, but not stopping.

" You mean—" Odom cursed suddenly. " Jehoso-phat ! And I wouldn't listen to you—couldn't see it—come on, if you think you can ride, let's get going. We'll fool them yet ! "

"I can ride all right, now," Scotty agreed, climbing back into the saddle. "Thanks, and—Odom—watch your step. You're as much a target as I am to-day."

Odom nodded, his lips set tight. Scotty took the hint and saved his breath. There was a tough ride ahead of them, and they both aimed to be in among the first three. Though his arm still throbbed the bleeding had been checked, and he could make the ride all right. In fact, he was still in about as good shape as the boss of the Quirt, if he was any judge. Those rides had shaken Jeff Odom up bad that morning, and he was in no shape for such a gruelling contest as still lay ahead.

Ahead was a meadow, spread out below them. Near the middle of it a ditch had been gashed sharply by a sudden cloudburst earlier in the year—a channel eight to ten feet deep and six to eight feet wide. Not a bad jump under ordinary circumstances. Jeff Odom was already setting his horse to it. Scotty saw him reach it, take off, he was across and out of sight around the shoulder of a hill.

Shaking his head to clear it, Scotty let Ten Spot have his head. This was all he needed for work like this. He settled himself in the saddle, felt the big horse rise, sail—then, as they struck, mud was sliding under the ploughing hoofs, sending horse and rider sprawling.

This time there was no chance to be ready, to fling himself off. Somehow, Scotty found himself out of the saddle and rolling in soft mud. Shaken but unhurt, he got to his feet, thankful that he hadn't landed on his wounded arm. Ten Spot, covered with mud, was up again, apparently unhurt as well by the fall.

A little further at the side, three or four other riders

had made the jump and thundered past. Hardly know-ing what he was about, Scotty climbed back in the saddle, pulling himself up with his good arm. Then he started on. He must be the last one now, with an almost unsurmountable handicap ahead.

But Ten Spot was eager to run. For the next few minutes, half dazed, riding mechanically, Scotty let him have his head. His own head was like his arm, pain-filled, not much good. Off at the side a bunch of cattle grazed, staring incuriously. Chokecherries, turning red under the sun, blushed at the ardency of its caress. Grass swished around Ten Spot's hoofs, his wounded arm throbbed and ached increasingly.

Ahead was another horse and rider. Shaking his head, Scotty watched the distance lessen, came along-side and drew gradually past. Here, where he could see for a couple of miles, other horses were spread out for almost the entire distance. He tried to count them, but his eyes seemed to blur. Most, if not nearly all of them, were in this length of open, however.

He overtook a second man, saw that it was one of those who had taken the lead at the start. The cayuse was labouring painfully, already spent. With over half the course still ahead, and that probably the toughest part.

Scotty's head cleared a little, and he steadied Ten Spot to a long, rolling gallop. The big pinto was run-ning almost as easily as at the start, not at all both-ered. But a few of those horses were still more than a mile ahead, and in all probability they were in good shape, too.

Here was rough country again, long, low hills, gashed by coulees, with occasional clumps of aspen or stunted, wind-twisted pine feathering their edges, brown buck-brush running down like a carpet, rose briars and the blue of serviceberry bushes in little knots and clumps. The course ran along old cow trails, skirting the edges of coulees, dropping to cross between ravines, climbing again, sometimes almost straight up. Back in here it was impossible to see far in any direction.

Three more riders had fallen behind the ground-eating lope of Ten Spot, which would mean that eight were still ahead. Scotty looked at his arm, saw that the bandage was bright with fresh blood, but it wasn't bleeding badly. Nor was it hurting much now, and the first weakness of it had left him. His head, for the first time since the shock of the bullet, was really clear again.

And this was excellent country for the killer to use for a second try. Having failed in his first attempt, he could cut straight across country, while the racers were compelled to follow the big circle, and with a good horse he would be here ahead of them. He might be somewhere up ahead again, now, determined to score a more direct hit the next time——

Scotty's narrowed eyes glinted. Two hundred yards ahead, a little to the right of the course, and some fifty feet above the trail, he had caught a gleam of light. A lance-like shaft of it which could be made only by a small movement of a rifle barrel, the sun rippling along it as it was moved. Up there the killer waited, much closer to the trail than he had been before. Having sighted Ten Spot and recognised the pinto, he was get-ting ready, like a puma crouching on a limb.

Just ahead was a clump of brush and trees. For a few moments it would hide horse and rider from sight of the gunman waiting up ahead. As they reached the shelter, Scotty swung Ten Spot farther to the right, down the fringe of another coulee which ran here like the spoke of a wheel out from the other. An old cattle trail ran here as well.

Shifting the reins to his left hand, Scotty gritted his teeth as he used his wounded arm, but hung on grimly. Slipping his right hand inside his shirt, he brought it out again, Colt at the ready.

By this time, of course, the killer crouching there in ambush was likely to be getting suspicious at his failure to keep coming along the cross-country trail, marked at the turns by little flags stuck up and easy to read. But, suspicious or not, Scotty knew that the killer would have no chance to change his plans, to get away.

Swinging through a patch of brush, small rocks rattled under Ten Spot's hoofs as he circled, climbing a steep slope. Then he had crested the rise, was bearing down on the spot where the gunman lurked.

The course for the race, down below, came in sight, with a horseman galloping along it. Then Scotty saw the lurking figure of the killer, crouching behind a natural barrier of grey-green boulders and rock currants, the bush growing stunted and wind-riven, almost the same hue as the rocks and the surrounding landscape.

Still intent on the trail below, the gunman stiffened alertly at sight of the other rider, the sun rippled again as the rifle moved. Then he relaxed again as it became apparent that this was not the man he wanted.

Suddenly, hearing a sound behind, the gunman swung about, swift amazement flowing across his face, to be wiped way by black hate as he recognised Scotty and saw how he had been caught in his own trap. Then he belatedly strove to bring his rifle up to his shoulder.

" Drop it, Tollard ! " Scotty snapped. " I've got you ! "

It was at that moment that one of the loose stones turned under Ten Spot's hoof, sending the pinto sliding wildly.

And in that instant the gun in Tollard's hands was belching flame and lead.

CHAPTER XXV

HOW LIGHTNING WAS STRUCK

IT WAS no particular surprise to Scotty to find that Tollard was the man who had tried to murder him before that day; the man was relentless in his hate, calculating as a puma in his method. Yet Scotty had had no intention, even with the drop on him, of shooting him down. Even when Tollard jerked his gun up again, he still preferred not to kill him.

Ten Spot had recovered almost at once from the loose stone under his hoof, but he was still quivering with the nervousness of that near-tumble. That, coupled with Tollard's sudden throwing of his own body sidewise, spoiled Scotty's aim for the big man's gun-arm. He heard the whistle of the rifle bullet past his ear, saw a flare of red seem to balloon out on Tollard's face as his own lead struck the nose, spraying upward in its course, dropping him before he knew what had hit him.

For a moment, with Ten Spot shivering at the gun-fire and snorting to the acrid tang of burned powder, Scotty stared down. This was too bad, in more ways than one. Alive, caught in such an act, Tollard might have been made to tell who was paying him for all this. Dead, he was past all telling.

So far as trying to murder Scotty was concerned, Tollard would have needed no urging. But his wanton attack on Mart Sullivan, weeks before, had probably not been due to chance, nor even the headlong rage of the moment.

Tollard had been a Diamond man then, and Mart belonged to the Quirt; such an attack could be calculated on to enhance the bitterness between the two outfits. Tollard's deliberate treachery towards the Diamond in the rodeo had certainly been schemed by a quicker brain than his, with pay for doing it.

Scotty started out of his reverie. Precious moments had been lost here, while the cross-country thundered on. The horseman who had inadvertently come so close to drawing one of Tollard's slugs had turned to stare over his shoulder for a moment at the blast of gun-fire, then had spurred harder than ever. Scotty swung the pinto down to the trail below, settled him to the run again.

It was a steady drag now, with every sort of hindrance placed there to thin out the contenders and to make this a race in the tough tradition of the Camas rodeos. Up hill and down, splashing across a creek, jumping ditches made by gouging water, now under the cool of pines, out again to boiling sun. For with the afternoon it had grown sultry, the air muggy and oppressive. Even Ten Spot was beginning to feel it, and lesser breeds of horses were fast playing out under the pace set by the leaders.

Only a couple more miles lay ahead now, with Camas soon to show around the corner of a low hill, and the end of the race in sight. Scotty's arm throbbed steadily, a burning lance of pain, and his head ached in tune with it. But over half of the starters were behind him. Ahead he could see Jeff Odom, galloping steadily, Mart Sullivan, and a third rider. His eyes narrowed, trying to figure something out, through the haze which tortured his brain. Now he had it. Where was Denton and his big black horse?

So far as he could remember he hadn't passed the black anywhere, yet Denton was nowhere to be seen. But something else was. A quarter of a mile ahead now was the worst hazard of the whole course—the old stone corral of the sheep herder, a line of brushing fringing it on one side, the slope of the hill leading down to it and narrowing it so that only one horse could make the jump at a time.

A treacherous place, with Jeff Odom riding now in the lead. Yet at every jump the gallant Ten Spot was narrowing the distance. There was little enough chance, however, Scotty knew, to overtake Jeff Odom in the distance remaining to the finish line.

Odom was riding as he had done that morning, seemingly immune to the punishment he had taken, determined to go on and win. Scotty gave him a grudging admiration. Whatever might be his faults he had plenty of nerve. He was steadying his horse as the wall loomed ahead when, without warning, the big

M

black horse shot out of the fringe of brush and thundered for the gap as well, the two horses racing shoulder to shoulder.

Scotty's mouth suddenly felt dry. One thing was only too plain now. The rider on the black had managed to get a lead on all of them, had easily had the chance to be across that treacherous wall before any other rider reached it, and to have gone on to victory in the race.

But he was in this race for a win of a different sort. So he had deliberately swung behind the screen of bushes, waiting for Jeff Odom—or, perhaps, Scotty, if he should be ahead—to come along. And now he was out to see that the boss of the Quirt did not finish the race.

By the time Odom saw him and realised the danger it was too late to check, too late to swerve. And both horses were thundering at the gap where there was room for only one horse at a time. Scotty heard Jeff Odom cry out, saw the big black swerve at him as the rider jerked at the reins, then Odom and his horse were down, a tangled heap at the foot of the wall, the black was across and thundering on.

White-faced, Mart Sullivan was swinging his horse out, checking to dismount and run to Odom's assistance. The other horse swerved wildly and was off at a tangent, out of the race. Scotty, teeth set, lifted Ten Spot to the jump, was across, and with Camas in sight at last, urging his horse on, in pursuit of the fleeing black.

He could see a blur of faces in the stands now, hear the excited voice of the crowd as they watched the finish. The black was three lengths ahead now—two lengths, as foot by foot, Ten Spot was creeping up on him, running fiercely, snorting at sight of any rival ahead. The man on the black was turning, staring back, then spurring desperately. But still Ten Spot was coming closer. Only a length separated them now; the roar of the crowd sounded loud in Scotty's ears.

Leaning forward, he spoke to Ten Spot, felt the pinto respond with an added burst of speed. Now his horse was at the black's tail. Inch by inch, foot by foot, he was coming up. At sight of this neck and neck finish, with Scotty Stemple riding, the crowd was going wild. Only a full half of it was imploring the man on the black to come on, to stop the Diamond from winning!

Scotty's jaw set grimly. Whichever of them won, it wouldn't take much to start trouble between the Diamond and the Quirt—especially when they learned what had happened to Jeff Odom back there. Unless he could tell them the truth before something else got going.

Ten Spot's nose was even with the black's shoulders now. He saw the black suddenly swerve in towards him, but he wasn't ready to be caught napping. He lifted Ten Spot a little to the side, was past, then they were crossing the finishing line, a length ahead.

Pandemonium had broken loose. Men were shouting, some cheering, others anxiously waiting for Odom, who was failing to appear. Scotty reined Ten Spot around; Dave Medwick was shouting for order. And then, above the quieting murmur, Si Denton, standing in the stirrups, was shouting.

" Judges, before you give that hombre the prize, listen tuh me! He'd ought tuh be disqualified for foul play. The man who'd have won would have been Jeff

Odom of the Quirt—if he hadn't fouled him back there
at the wall, so that Odom's horse fell on him! "

CHAPTER XXVI

DIAMOND DAY

THE hush following that charge held for a moment
but it was a different kind of silence now, the calm
before the storm. Quirt men and Diamond were drawing apart, restless hands were hovering poised for swift
descent on guns. Here, unless he could stop it, Scotty
saw, was what this man had been playing for all along,
the spark to set off dynamite and send both sides tearing like mad dogs at each other's throats.

It was up to him to stop it—and do it quick. There
might be one way—and he wouldn't have to pretend
very much, at that.

"Folks," he drawled, and both hands, they could
see, were now clutched tight on the big saddle horn,
" after ridin' in the bucking, this morning, and now in
the cross-country, I know it sounds plumb unheroic—
but unless I get a drink pretty pronto, I'm going to
faint like one of these heroines you read about."

He was swaying in the saddle, white-faced. Men
stared, and some of the tenseness, the animosity of a
moment before melted. They could see now that he
was plastered with dried mud, that his arm was bandaged and the cloth wet with fresh blood. Two or three

pressed forward with offers of flasks, one man held out a tin cup of water. A Quirt man. Scotty took it, drank slowly, and passed it back.

"Thanks," he said. "That helps. Now, if I can get my feet on terra firmy again——"

Still clinging to the horn, he descended laboriously to the ground, making a show of it. Denton was watching him with the rest, undecided, his plan upset by this new development. Now he swung down as well.

"A man that'd foul another rider, to tumble a horse on him, deserves tuh feel somethin' more than faint!" he growled.

The fire was smouldering redly, and it wouldn't take much to fan it to flame. They'd given Scotty the drink he asked for, allowed him a minute's time. But their patience was running out like the draining sand in an hour glass. He had to have something else—have it quick. And then his eye lighted.

"I might tell you my side of it," he said. "But right now that would be a waste of words. Here's something that's a lot better argument. This hombre ain't got his whiskers stuck down good. They're curlin' up at one corner."

Two sudden strides carried him to Denton. Still speaking, and before even Denton himself quite understood his intention, Scotty's hand struck, jerked back. With it came most of the whiskers and, at that transformation, even Scotty stared in amazement. For the man beneath the disguise was Pop.

And on his right cheek, which had been hidden by the whiskers, was a sharp, deep cut—and this one, unlike the mark on Bill Winters' face, Scotty knew had not been forged there by a knife blade. It had been cut by his diamond the night before.

"Why, danged if it ain't Pop Blayley!" someone swore in astonishment.

"Blayley!" Scotty swung, eyes narrowed. He remembered now that he had never heard anyone mention Pop's last name, had never thought much about it up to now. Blayley! That explained a lot. The same jovial way as Blayley of the Lazy Azey—the same general build, and all. Only Pop was a considerably older man. But at last the pieces in the puzzle were falling into place.

"He's done his talking," Scotty rapped out. "Doing it behind a disguise, like he's done a lot of other things. Right now, I'm going to speak my piece——"

Without seeming to notice what was happening, Scotty spun suddenly, his fingers darted out, clamped down on Pop's hand as a six-gun flashed in the sun. He twisted, the weapon clattered on the ground. Still holding the futilely struggling Pop in a grip like that of a bear trap, Scotty went on.

"Sheriff, grab Blayley there. I'm charging him with the murder of Bill Winters. Now the rest of you folks listen. This row isn't between the Quirt and the Diamond. Both outfits have been used for cat's-paws to pull chestnuts——"

"What about Jeff Odom?" someone yelled. "Did yuh foul him back there?"

Scotty's head jerked around for a swift look. Relief was in his eyes, but it did not show in his face or alter the clipped tone of his voice.

"There comes Jeff now, along with Mart Sullivan. Looks like he wasn't bad hurt, after all. It was Pop

Blayley, posing as Denton, who crowded him back there at the jump. Ask Jeff himself."

There was a murmur in the crowd, but they were undecided now, and curious. Jeff Odom was coming up with Mart Sullivan, on another horse. A smear of blood on his cheek, his torn and muddy clothes lent him a wild, dishevelled appearance, but it was plain enough that he hadn't been bad hurt. He rode straight up beside Scotty, reined up and looked over the crowd.

"I heard what was just said," he nodded. "Scotty's right. It was Denton who fouled me. Broke the back of my Lightning horse, so we had to shoot him. I was lucky—a lot more than I deserve to be, looks like, after the fool I've been lately."

"No more so than most of us, Jeff," Scotty said quietly. "I've been pretty much fooled, myself. This morning I figured that Blayley was back of this, but I still didn't suspect Pop. Blayley's his son, of course. And Pop, posing as a saddle tramp, going everywhere, has been the brains of this scheme. And has worked it mighty smooth, with all that he knew about every outfit, gained from visiting among them."

Jeff Odom dismounted wearily. He staggered, threw one arm across Scotty's shoulders to steady himself.

"I'm backin' whatever Scotty says," he pronounced. "I don't know much about it all yet. But he does."

"It's pretty simple," Scotty explained. "There's coal on the Quirt and the Diamond—a big vein of it, and a fortune right there, with the railroad coming—not to mention what both ranches are worth to start with.

"There wasn't any way of getting possession of any of that in a straight, honest way, so the Blayleys made this play for it—to build up a feud between the two big outfits, and with this rodeo for the payoff. It was aimed that both would lose on the bet, and the stranger, Si Denton, held the bets. If anything went wrong with that scheme, you were to be set to fighting, and in the free-for-all, they still figured to come out on top.''

"Gosh, it was mighty close tuh that, Scotty," someone boomed. "If yuh hadn't pulled that one about bein' un-heeroic, and near faintin' on us, there'd a been plenty gun-smoke hangin' like a fog over Camas right now."

Scotty grinned faintly.

"That was right close to the truth," he grunted. "Still is. I guess you can fill in the details by yourselves. Way it shapes up, I figure all bets are off, which is the best way."

He stopped suddenly as Dawn Sullivan hurried up to them, her cheeks flushed. One of the deputy sheriffs had led the now silent Pop away, alongside Blayley. Dawn shot a questioning look from Jeff to Scotty.

"Are you boys hurt?" she demanded, cried out then at sight of Scotty's bandaged and bloody arm.

"That's nothing much," Scotty explained. "Just a hole through the flesh. Didn't touch a bone. And Jeff tied it up for me."

"Who—who did it?" Her eyes were big.

"Some hombre shot from ambush," Jeff Odom growled. "It must have been either Pop or Blayley——"

Scotty shook his head.

"It was Tollard, Jeff. He tried it again—and made a little mistake. I reckon he was taking their pay, though we won't be able to prove that. But there's plenty against them as it is."

Jeff Odom hesitated a moment, his face reddening. Then he held out his hand.

"I've been a fool all along, Scotty. But now—well, if you've a mind to shake and forget it, I'm willing to admit that you're a better man than I am, feller."

"One man's better in some things, and another in other lines," Scotty retorted, gripping the proffered hand heartily. "I've always kind of liked you, Jeff, even if we did keep tanglin'."

"I forgot to tell you," Dawn said suddenly. "I just came from your friend, Fatty. He's better, Scotty."

"Why, that's right encouragin' news," Scotty admitted. "Guess I'll have to be runnin' along and have a look at him. See you both later."

It was Jeff Odom's hand on his shoulder that checked him. Odom's face was nearly as red as his hair, but he contrived to smile a little.

"Don't be a fool and run off that way, Scotty. I was a fool—last night. But any way you take it, Dawn's nerves have been stretched pretty bad, these last few days, and she likely wants to cry on a shoulder to relieve 'em. And yours is the only shoulder that'll do. Like I said before, you're a better man than I am."

He turned suddenly, was gone. The crowd had thinned out, leaving them alone. It was Scotty's turn to redden as he met Dawn's gaze.

"Dawn," he said uncertainly. "I figured——"

"Yes?" She wasn't looking at him now, and he gathered courage.

"I—Fatty, or Pop, or somebody, told me that you were engaged—engaged to be wedded—to Jeff——"

She glanced up for a moment.

"Pop always was an awful liar, Scotty."

Scotty stared for a moment, still incredulous. Then he remembered that he still had one good arm.

A few minutes later, absentmindedly, his fingers encountered a lump in his vest pocket. He felt of it, and a slow smile overspread his face.

"Golly," he reflected. "Reckon I won't have to turn this diamond back, after all. Just get it shifted around to a different ring, and it'll be serving a better purpose than ever. Why, doggone it, this sure seems to be Diamond day!"